MW01061536

by

Aury Wallington

razOr
bill

Pop!

RAZORBILL

Published by the Penguin Group
Penguin Young Readers Group
345 Hudson Street, New York, New York 10014, U.S.A.
Penguin Group (USA) Inc., 375 Hudson Street,
New York, New York 10014, U.S.A.
Penguin Group (Canada), 90 Eglinton Avenue East, Suite 700, Toronto, Ontario, Canada
M4P 2Y3 (a division of Pearson Penguin Canada Inc.)
Penguin Books Ltd, 80 Strand, London WC2R 0RL, England
Penguin Ireland, 25 St Stephen's Green, Dublin 2, Ireland
(a division of Penguin Books Ltd)
Penguin Group (Australia), 250 Camberwell Road, Camberwell,
Victoria 3124, Australia (a division of Pearson Australia Group Pty Ltd)
Penguin Books India Pvt Ltd, 11 Community Centre, Panchsheel Park,
New Delhi – 110 017, India
Penguin Group (NZ), Cnr Airborne and Rosedale Roads, Albany,
Auckland 1310, New Zealand (a division of Pearson New Zealand Ltd)
Penguin Books (South Africa) (Pty) Ltd, 24 Sturdee Avenue, Rosebank,
Johannesburg 2196, South Africa

Penguin Books Ltd, Registered Offices: 80 Strand, London WC2R 0RL, England

10 9 8 7 6 5 4 3 2 1

Copyright 2006 © Aury Wallington
All rights reserved

Library of Congress Cataloging-in-Publication Data

Wallington, Aury.
    Pop! / by Aury Wallington.
        p. cm.
    Summary: When seventeen-year-old Marit decides to lose her virginity to
her best friend, she finds that separating sex from love proves to be more
complicated than she expected.
    ISBN 1-59514-092-1
    [1. Sex—Fiction. 2. Best friends—Fiction. 3. Friendship—Fiction. 4.
Dating (Social customs)—Fiction.]   I. Title.
    PZ7.W159363Po 2006
    [Fic]—dc22

                                        2006013016

Printed in the United States of America

The scanning, uploading and distribution of this book via the Internet or via any other
means without the permission of the publisher is illegal and punishable by law. Please
purchase only authorized electronic editions, and do not participate in or encourage electronic piracy of copyrighted materials. Your support of the author's rights is appreciated.

The publisher does not have any control over and does not assume any responsibility for
author or third-party websites or their content.

To Natalie . . . in a few years

Prologue

They knew. I was sure of it.

The waiter who took our dinner order. The couple at the next table. The people we walked past on our way into the restaurant.

All night long, I was positive that everyone could tell, just by looking at me, that before the night was out, I would no longer be the only seventeen-year-old virgin left in Connecticut.

The only person oblivious to that fact? The guy with whom I was going to do it.

"So, how'd you like the movie?" Eric asked, holding my hand across the table.

We were at Mona Lisa, an Italian restaurant right near the Greenwich Country Club. Usually I love the place, but tonight it barely registered. We could have been eating hot dogs out of a Dumpster for all it mattered. Tonight I was going to have *sex*. And until that happened, I couldn't concentrate on anything else.

"Yeah," I said, not really answering. I was too preoccupied with the way Eric was rubbing his thumb *back and forth* across the top of my hand. I'm sure he thought it was romantic, but actually, it was kind of . . . chafing.

I looked closely at Eric's thumb. It was red and dry. You could see clearly where each individual black hair sprouted out of his skin.

I was pretty sure I had seen Eric's thumbs before. So why, tonight, did they look so . . . *blech?*

I pulled my hand away and poured some more Diet Coke into my glass. I crunched a few ice cubes while Eric smiled.

"You know what they say about chewing your ice," he said.

"What?" I asked.

Eric leaned in and whispered, "Same thing they say about green M&M's."

I gasped. So he *did* know!

Did that make me feel better or worse?

I took another sip of my drink, careful not to get any ice in my mouth this time.

Eric picked up his own glass and crunched a few of his

own ice cubes. I couldn't decide if that made him funny or a big jerk.

"So how's school?" I asked him.

Eric went to St. Bernard's. They started classes two whole weeks before we did.

"Man, my morality teacher is so cool," Eric said. "Sister Marguerite. She started telling us about all these cases of bioethics, like a family who had a second kid because their first one needed a bone marrow transplant, and what are the ethics of doing something like that? She doesn't talk like a nun at all. She lets us make up our own minds about things. You know?"

"My mom had a case like that," I told him.

My mom is chief legal counsel for Greenwich Memorial Hospital. She always has crazy stories about the trouble the patients and doctors get into.

"There was this woman who already had three kids, and she—"

"Yeah, and there was this other guy, who had been on life support for years, right? He was a total vegetable—" The pizza arrived, and Eric reached out and grabbed a slice. "Anyway, his family wanted to pull the plug because he was completely brain-dead, but his wife didn't want to let him go, right?"

Eric took a huge bite of pizza. He chewed for a moment—then his eyes went wide. His face turned bright red.

"What's the matter?" I asked.

He opened his mouth, giving me a close-up view of mangled sauce, cheese, and crust. He fanned at his tongue, making "hot hot hot" noises. Then he spat the big chunk of pizza onto his plate.

I winced.

Eric gulped some of his drink before saying, "Ow! Sorry." He wrapped the half-chewed bit up in his napkin, took another, smaller bite, and continued his story from where he left off.

I slid a piece of pizza onto my own plate and silently waited for it to cool down. While I waited, Eric babbled on. And on. And on.

This is it, I thought. *This is the magical evening I'll always remember. The one I'll cherish and compare to all subsequent evenings. Eric, with his red, hairy thumbs, endless stories, and spit-out pizza, will be with me forever.*

Hmmm.

Eric finished raving about Sister Marguerite and barely took a breath before launching into a story about his chemistry teacher, Brother Jonah. I watched his mouth moving and his hands gesturing in the air. I ate two pieces of pizza and picked all the toppings off a third.

Too late, I realized I probably shouldn't have gone for that last slice. It made me feel too full to be seen without my clothes on.

I gulped. Without my clothes on . . .

Well, at least the car would be dark.

Pop!

As I thought of Eric's car—and what would go on in that car post-pizza—tiny beads of sweat began to form on my forehead.

I scolded myself. Why was I so nervous? Eric had been a good boyfriend in the couple of months since we'd started dating. There was no way I could chicken out now.

So, I decided, whatever. Full speed ahead.

Eric paid the check, and I wrapped my arm around his waist as we walked out to the car. I slipped my hand into his back pocket, and when he asked what we should do next, I said, "Let's go somewhere we can be alone."

We got into his mom's Saab station wagon and drove out to East Rock Park. Eric pulled down a leafy little lane heading toward the Pop Warner clubhouse and put the car in park.

It was a steamy night, so we had the windows down. Eric slid a cassette into the tape player and moved closer to me.

"You're so beautiful," he murmured, and put his hands on my face as he kissed me.

Sigh. I am a sucker for boys who touch my face during lip lock. It is the rare specimen who realizes that kissing isn't only about the mouth.

Eric's hands wandered down my neck and, slowly, through my hair. I kissed him back, shutting my eyes and trying not to think about the next twenty minutes.

About how I was going to get from kissing in the front seat to emerging from the backseat a Woman.

Eric stopped for a moment, tilted back his head, and smiled at me. "Hi," he said softly. Then he leaned in, pressing me back against my seat. His wristwatch snagged on my hair and pulled it.

Ow! I shut my eyes again and tried to get into it, tried to enjoy the faint spicy flavor of his tongue slipping into my mouth, but after a while, all I could feel was the hot air whooshing out of his nose and spreading over my face.

I opened my eyes, hoping to make an adjustment, and saw straight up one of Eric's nostrils. It was full of black hairs, just like his thumb, and . . .

Wait. Was that . . . ?

Ugh! Hadn't anyone ever taught him to use a tissue?

At that moment, it was official: Any trace of desire I felt for Eric went screaming out the window.

Moment: ruined.

Intentions: thwarted.

Chance at de-virginization: completely, utterly over.

I put my hands on Eric's shoulders, lightly pushing him away.

"Marit," he gasped. The wheezy, sexy tone of his voice made a thousand tiny ants crawl over my skin. "I want you so bad."

"Yeah," I said, sitting up a little straighter. "Sorry. But I gotta go."

y life is total suckola," I moaned, clutching my head in my hands.

The bell hadn't rung on the first day of school, but already I knew the year was hopeless.

Caroline and Jamie exchanged amused glances.

"What's wrong?" Jamie asked in mock alarm. "Did you forget to bring lip gloss with you? Is someone else carrying the *exact same* backpack? Did you just realize that your earrings don't match your socks?"

Caroline held back a laugh. "Dude, I can lend you some gloss, but if it's the earring thing? I'm afraid that's between you and Mr. Blackwell here."

She gestured toward Jamie, who shook his head sadly.

"First of all," I said, poking my fingers through the holes

in Jamie's fraying T-shirt, "there's nothing wrong with taking a bit of care with one's appearance—"

"Those holes are a statement," he protested. "It's retro grunge."

"Second, lip gloss is so not what I'm upset about. Eric and I"—I paused to make sure they were paying attention—"Eric and I broke up last night."

I hung my head low and opened my arms for the hugs of consolation that were due to me.

But there were no hugs forthcoming. My arms hung mid-air. I stood there, looking like some kind of demented scarecrow.

I glanced up. Jamie and Caroline gaped at me, their expressions blank.

"Didn't you hear what I said?" I asked. "Eric and I are finished. Over! I'm never going to see him again."

I stuck my arms out again. This time more forcefully.

Still, just vacant stares. I dropped my arms to my sides.

"You guys," I wailed. "My heart is broken!"

"It is not," Caroline said. "You never liked Eric to begin with."

"Yes, I did!" I said, shocked. "From the moment I met him, I knew that—"

"You met him 'cause he dropped a Fudgsicle in your lap,"

Jamie reminded me. "He's a walking calamity. Living proof of the theory of evolution. In fact, I believe it was you who said, 'The fry guy at McDonald's better be worried, because as soon as Eric graduates, he's going to set the world of fast food on fire . . .'"

"'. . . unless he sets the restaurant on fire first!'" Caroline finished, cracking up.

Okay, so Eric wasn't exactly the smoothest operator around. And whenever we went out, I was sure to end up rolling my eyes at his, shall we say, *lack of poise*. One time, I actually lost a contact. But still . . .

"I just—I thought that things between us might work out, you know? I thought he was going to be *the one*."

"The one what?" Jamie asked.

"The one—everything. We'd have sex. Fall in love. Go to prom."

"Prom. It's a stupid tradition, and what's the point?" Caroline said in a Molly Ringwald voice.

Caroline and I are obsessed with *Pretty in Pink*. We watch it at least once a week. Jamie makes fun of us for liking it— he's a total film snob. But he always hangs around whenever we shove the disc into the DVD player. We're pretty sure that deep down, he loves Molly as much as we do.

"Besides, it's senior year! Our last year together," Caroline reminded me. "Boys just complicate things. That's why I'm swearing off them. You don't want to be tied down with some lame boyfriend when you could out be having fun with me and Jamie, do you?"

I couldn't help it. I snorted.

"What was that for?" Caroline asked.

"Easy for *you* to say," I told her. "Every guy you meet falls head over heels in love with you."

Caroline is my friend, make no mistake about it. But she's like a little pixie—all tiny and blue-eyed and perfect. Guys practically line up to ask her out. If she wasn't so cool, I'm certain I'd feel compelled to hate her.

Me? Even in flip-flops, I tower over every boy in school.

And there are, of course, my other impediments—dark, impossible hair that curls in about a thousand different directions, paler-than-pale skin with the bluish-white tinge of skim milk . . .

It all adds up to guys *not* throwing themselves at my feet in the hallways of Sterling Prep. At least, not purposely.

"Eric was my only shot at having a boyfriend this year." I groaned. "*Now* who am I supposed to go out with? No one here at Sterling is even remotely interested in me."

"Marit, that's crazy talk." Jamie slung a comforting arm across my shoulders. "Any guy at this school would kill to go out with you."

I frowned, disbelieving. "Really? Then how come no one ever asks?"

"They're intimidated," Jamie answered promptly. "You're so gorgeous, you're unapproachable. Tell me, how does it feel being the hottest person in the room?"

"Must be a lot of pressure," Caroline observed, "even without the glossy lips."

"Stop," I said with a smile. And even though I was still as boyfriendless as I had been moments before, somehow I felt a little better.

Let me tell you a little bit about Jamie, Caroline, and me. We have been best friends for literally ever.

Caroline has lived next door to me since we were five, and her parents are crazy. I mean, certifiable. They keep separating and getting back together, over and over. She never knows when she gets home from school if her dad is living with her that day or not. To escape the asylum, she spends all her free time at my house.

My parents? Totally boring. They never, ever fight. That's why, when my older sister, Hilly, graduated high school last year, Caroline and I came up with a plan. Caroline would move into Hilly's bedroom and live with us. Then her parents could call up and make appointments to see her on the days they weren't throwing plates at each other. It was the perfect solution to Caroline's parental woes.

Unfortunately, Hilly screwed up—in tremendous fashion. She had her heart so dead set on going to Georgetown that she didn't bother to apply to any other colleges. When Georgetown rejected her, she was stuck living at home for a year, applying to other colleges while alternately sulking in her room and working at Nine West.

In addition to becoming Connecticut's poster child for safety schools, Hilly also wrecked Caroline's friendly takeover of her bedroom. So Caroline made do with coming over after school every single day, just the way she always had.

I first met Jamie in fourth-grade strings class. In our school, everyone has to learn an instrument, and the two of us were assigned the violin. We were so bad at it that while the rest of the class tackled Chopin, the two of us were sent to a rehearsal room to practice clapping in four-four time.

Jamie started coming over every day to practice the violin. Five minutes later Caroline would show up. Before we knew it, the three of us were inseparable.

Jamie and I are what you might call artsy types. We favor black clothes; we like our music alternative. Caroline's more mainstream. She's even been known to sport the occasional burst of pink—but I guess when you live in a crazy house, you want everything else in your life to be as completely normal as possible.

That is my life, thus far, with my friends. I love them, but I want more to my social life. I want romance. I want excitement. I want a *boyfriend*.

And now I don't know where I'm going to find one.

really thought Eric and I would last," I told Jamie and Caroline as we strolled into homeroom.

Jamie groaned. "Are we still talking about this?"

"Marit," Caroline said gently, "*none* of your boyfriends last."

"I know!" I whimpered. "And I can't figure out why."

Jamie and Caroline exchanged a glance.

"What?" I demanded.

"Um, haven't you noticed that there's kind of a . . . pattern to your breakups?" Jamie asked.

I thought about it. "Not really. I just know that I get myself all worked up liking a guy, and then things fall apart."

"Yes, but *when* do they fall apart?" Caroline asked, giving me a significant look.

"Beats me. When he starts acting like a jerk?" I guessed.

"Or when you . . ." She made a cryptic gesture with her hands, then sat back, looking pleased with either her psychological astuteness or her miming skills.

"When I *what*?"

Jamie and Caroline exchanged another glance, and it was all I could do not to knock their heads together like a pair of coconuts. "What?!"

Caroline rolled her eyes. "You always dump a guy as soon as things get physical."

I blinked. That wasn't what I was expecting to hear. "That's not true! I don't do that," I argued.

"You do," Caroline insisted. "Every single time."

"No way. That's crazy."

"Marit, think about it," Jamie said, slipping into a nearby desk. "Anytime you date a guy for more than a month, you start to get all freaky and uncomfortable. The next thing you know, you're single again."

Caroline was nodding so vigorously, I wouldn't have been surprised if she snapped a few vertebrae.

"Exactly!" she crowed. "You're afraid of sex!"

I cringed, then whispered, attempting to keep the conversation at an appropriate volume. "Oh my God. What are you talking about? I'm *dying* to have sex. I *can't wait* to have sex. I'm certainly not afraid of it."

"You are!" Caroline insisted. "Look, you've had, what, four boyfriends?"

"Five," I corrected.

She did a quick count on her fingers. "Eric, Alex, Louis, Hunter—who's the fifth?"

"Nicky Coleman."

Caroline let out a dismissive little chuckle. "You can't count Nicky."

"Why not? He was my first love."

"But you were eleven! You never even kissed! Which, come to think of it, proves my point. You broke up with *all* those guys as soon as things started getting physical."

"That can't be right," I protested weakly, but my mind was reeling. Did I do that? I frowned, considering. . . .

Nicky was my sixth-grade sweetheart. We never actually went out on a date, but he would stop by my table at lunch every day and give me half of his dessert or a bag of Cheetos or something.

And once we sat next to each other at a Stranger Danger assembly. He hooked his pinky around mine as the lights went down and kept it there until we were dismissed back to class.

Things were heaven between Nicky and me until that fateful day they gave the sixth graders The Talk. Boys were herded off to the gym, while we girls shuffled over to the auditorium to hear the Plain Facts about periods and boys and "no means no."

Pop!

The problem wasn't so much what the school nurse *said* during The Talk—I'd heard all that before, from my older sister. But the publicness of it was unbearable.

And the thought of *doing* any of the things she talked about—when every girl in my class now knew the clinical terms for them? Well, it was just too disturbing.

I could not keep encouraging Nicky's affection when, obviously, I was going to have to become a nun. I broke things off that afternoon.

Hunter came next, when I was thirteen. At that point I'd gotten over being freaked out by sex ed, and Hunter and I would kiss every chance we got. We had been together three weeks when it all went south.

By eighth grade most of the girls in my class had started wearing bras, even though the majority of them didn't need them yet.

Let's just say I needed one. Boy, did I need one.

By the time I turned thirteen, I was filling a C cup. It was completely mortifying, and even though my mom swore that one day I would appreciate being "perfectly proportioned," I was hypersensitive. I didn't want anyone to notice my boobs—especially Hunter.

Around the same time the girls were starting to get boobs, the boys were figuring out new ways to torture us. The hands-down favorite method? Snapping bras.

17

And while I'm sure it was annoying and embarrassing for the girls in AA training bras when someone snuck up on them in the hallway, I strapped myself into a big old honking Olga minimizer every morning. It had three rows of hooks in the back and enough elastic to shrink-wrap half the school. The first time a boy snapped my bra, it left a welt that didn't go away for *hours.*

So I took to walking down the halls sideways, with my back pressed against the lockers, to keep it from happening again.

Of course, this only added fuel to the fire. It was so clear that I wanted to avoid having my bra snapped that it became the chief pursuit of practically every boy in school.

I upped my defenses—wearing a thick parka over my clothes all day so boys couldn't get a handhold. I enlisted Jamie or Caroline to walk directly behind me at all times, with strict instructions to break the fingers of anyone who reached for me.

And it worked—I remained snap free, until the day Hunter stopped me after school and asked me if I wanted to go to the Snowflake dance. I was so excited, I threw my arms around him and gave him a hug.

He hugged me back, his arms encircling me, holding me tight. And just when I thought I would burst with happiness, his hands wandered to the center of my back, grabbed my bra strap, and—*snap!*

Pop!

Needless to say, I didn't go to the dance with Hunter. I didn't go anywhere with him, ever again.

My boobs were the cause of my breakup with my third boyfriend too. It was during a slow dance at the Sophomore Spring Formal. Louis and I were swaying to Usher's "U Got It Bad," and out of nowhere he put his hand on the front of my dress, right on top of my boob. It startled me so badly I let out a yelp and jumped back about three feet.

Louis looked at me like I was a lunatic. "You okay?"

"Yeah. Sorry," I said, moving back into his arms and trying to pick up the rhythm. "You just—surprised me is all."

"Sorry," he said, then he moved his hand so it was hovering about a centimeter over my chest. "Do you mind if I—"

I blushed, too shy to meet his eyes, and gave a little shrug. "Whatever," I mumbled, and he set his hand back down.

I guess it felt okay—I mean, it wasn't exactly rocking my world, but it didn't gross me out.

I couldn't imagine that Louis was getting much of a thrill out of it either, but when I looked at him, he had his eyes shut and a dreamy smile on his face.

He nuzzled his nose in my ear, then whispered, "Your boobs are so big."

I stiffened, horrified. "Are you kidding?"

"No. They're enormous. Like . . . like two sexy pillows."

"God, shut up," I said. I grabbed his hand and moved it

back to my shoulder. My whole body flushed warm and suddenly it was hard to breathe.

Louis opened his eyes, surprised and annoyed. "Hey, what's your problem?"

My problem was that I felt like a freak, and any attention to my deformities made me want to lock myself in my bedroom forever.

And besides . . . sexy *pillows*?

It was mortifying, but there was no way I was telling Louis that.

Instead I punched him. Right there on the dance floor.

Next contestant, please?

Alex and I started going out the day after I turned sixteen. We broke up because we were making out on the couch in his basement when he let out a little gasp, jumped up really quickly, and ran into the bathroom.

I only knew what had happened because I saw the same thing in an episode of *Everwood*.

I also knew that once Alex cleaned himself up, there was no way I'd be able to face him without either bursting into a fit of hysterical laughter . . . or tears. So I straightened my shirt, grabbed my backpack, and by the time Alex got back to the couch, I had already disappeared.

That brought me to Eric. And honestly, I defy anyone to

stay "in the mood" after they've seen the crusty critters living inside *those* nostrils.

But as much as I hated to admit it, Jamie and Caroline had a point. Every single one of those relationships had been ruined by an attempt to get physical.

Oh my God. Was I really afraid of sex?

"This is terrible!" I groaned. "I'm—I'm an *ice queen!*"

"You are not an ice queen," Jamie said. "You're just—selective."

"Besides," Caroline put in. "*Anybody* would be repulsed by the guys you've dated."

"Thanks," I said, making a face. Then I stopped short. "But you guys, what if I found the perfect guy, like, tomorrow? Personality, looks—a total eleven. What happens then? Are you telling me I'll blow it the instant things start getting serious?"

Caroline just looked at me, her eyes pitying.

I put my head in my hands. "I'll *never* have a decent relationship. Ever."

"Sure, you will," Jamie said, punching me on the shoulder.

"I won't," I insisted. "Sex is a part of any long-term relationship, and I'm too afraid to have it! I'm already the only virgin in school!"

Caroline blew out an exasperated breath. "Marit, you are *not.*"

"Yeah? Name another," I challenged.

She put a finger to her lips, pretending to think hard. "Hmmm, who could it be?" she asked. "Oh, wait! I know—*Jamie.*"

Jamie pulled Caroline's Billabong hoodie up over her head. "Thanks. Thanks for bringing that up."

It was true—Jamie and I were the only virgins left at Sterling Prep. And deep down, I knew that Jamie's capital *V* bothered him too. He just . . . hid it better.

And it isn't like Jamie's hideous—even with his red hair, which I personally think is a shame on a boy. He just has this rumpled, intellectual hipster thing going, which doesn't attract the glamor girls who make up most of the Sterling student body.

Hmmm. When I thought about it, Jamie and I really *were* in the same boat.

"What's the big deal anyway?" Caroline asked, tilting her head back to see from under her giant hood. "Better to be a virgin than do it with the wrong guy. Sex sucks if you aren't in love."

She paused, then added softly, "Just look at my parents."

Jamie and I exchanged a panicked look.

Caroline reached into her backpack and calmly took out a notebook and pen.

Slowly, I let out a breath.

Crisis averted. Caroline's parents were separated—this week. And when it came to discussing them, she could get explosive—quickly.

The bell rang then and Mrs. Popham, our homeroom teacher, called the class to order. She gave us the usual "welcome back" speech, then passed out a blizzard of locker assignments, permission slips, emergency forms, and class schedules.

I was filling out my "student information sheet" when I was struck by a thought. This was the very last first day of high school I would ever have. And before high school was through, I wanted a real boyfriend. I wanted a real relationship. And if I was going to have one and hold on to him, I had to do something.

More specifically, I had to get over my fear of doing "it."

And fast.

s this some sort of sick joke?" I asked, staring down at the piece of paper in my hand.

"Maybe we offended someone in the administration office," Caroline said. "Maybe we're being punished."

Jamie shut his eyes and leaned back against his locker. People swirled around us, on their way to their first class of the new year.

"Worst. Schedule. Ever." He groaned.

"Second-period lunch?" I asked. "This has got to be a mistake. I can't have lunch at nine in the morning!"

"Oh my God, you guys. Fourth-period gym?" Caroline wailed. "Do you know how much time it takes me to get my hair and makeup right in the morning? And they expect me get all sweaty in the middle of the day? No. I just won't do it."

"We don't exactly have a choice," I pointed out.

"Oh yes, we do," Caroline argued. "They can't make me sweat if I don't want to. I'll—I'll say I have cramps."

"Yeah, like Ms. Vandermeer is going to let that stop you." I lowered my voice and squared my shoulders in what I thought was a pretty decent imitation. "Exercise releases endorphins. That'll make those cramps hit the road, jack!"

Caroline dropped her head. "This is a disaster."

"Welcome to senior year," Jamie said.

The bell rang for first period, and Caroline headed off to drama class. Jamie and I made our way to the temporary building that housed the band room.

The first day of orchestra is always tense, with everyone having to sight-read a section of whatever our conductor, Mr. Murphy, is currently enamored with. It's a mini-audition to determine who will land the coveted "first chair" for their instrument.

In the seven years Jamie and I have been tackling the violin, neither of us has managed to produce anything remotely resembling a melody, so we are happily resigned to our end-of-the-row sixth- and seventh-chair positions. We used to challenge each other for sixth chair on a regular basis, but Mr. Murphy finally threw up his hands and said we were tied for last, so it didn't matter who sat where.

While the other kids were nervously studying their sheet

music and applying rosin to their bows, Jamie and I slouched back against the percussion section and tried to talk softly.

"This year is not going according to plan," I muttered.

Jamie snickered. "You're that upset about second-period lunch?"

"No. I'm upset that I apparently have a *giant phobia* about sex, which you and Caroline were aware of all along."

Jamie stuck out his tongue and made a gagging sound. "Come on, Marit. It's not that big a deal."

"It *is* a big deal! How am I ever going to have a boyfriend if I'm so freaked out about sex that I never have sex at all?"

Jamie considered. "Well, you're aware of your problem now. So, like, maybe if you go out with a guy and start to act all weird, you'll recognize what you're doing—and stop doing it."

I considered this for a moment. "Do you really think that could work?"

He nodded. "Definitely. The first step to fixing a problem is admitting you *have* a problem."

For the first time that day, hope bubbled up inside me. "And after I've done it once, the problem is solved, right? Because as soon as I'm *not* a virgin, I won't have to freak about losing my virginity anymore."

"Right. The pressure's off," Jamie said. "But Marit?"

"Yeah?"

"Don't get back together with Eric, okay? He's not good enough to be your first time."

I grinned at Jamie. "Not a chance. I'm admitting I have a problem—with trying to lose my virginity to a guy whose nostrils are big enough to drive Volkswagen through."

Jamie let out a bark of laughter, which made Mr. Murphy glare at us.

"So, do you think it worked?" I asked when Mr. Murphy had turned away. "Am I cured of Eric-itis?"

"Let's see. Does this turn you on?" Jamie pushed his nose up with his fingers so I could see inside his nostrils. He moved his face toward mine like he was going to kiss me or, more likely, wipe boogers on me.

I shrieked and pushed him away, and we both collapsed into our seats, trying to stifle our giggles.

We were the first people in the cafeteria at lunchtime, so we snagged the completely prime table by the courtyard, laying claim to it as ours for the duration of the school year.

Where you sit at lunch can make or break your whole day. Most of the tables are banked against the glass wall that separates the cafeteria from the administration offices, and nothing kills your appetite like trying to choke down a pizza bagel with the school secretaries glaring at you or principal-bound delinquents giving you the finger through the glass.

There are only two tables in the entire cafeteria where you can get a bit of privacy, and landing one of them was the first good thing about senior year.

"Oh no, you too?" a voice called.

I turned and found our buds Nina and Abby entering the cafeteria. We shoved over to give them room, and they dropped into chairs next to us.

"Second-period lunch." Nina sighed. "I thought being a senior was supposed to have its privileges."

"Ugh. This is disgusting." Caroline groaned, picking at her hot dog and Tater Tots. "It's too early to eat this kind of food."

I had to agree. Then a thought occurred to me. "Hey, if we don't ever feel like eating lunch, maybe we'll lose weight without having to diet!"

Abby immediately put down her hot dog. "That? Is genius."

"We're actually *lucky* to have gotten second-period lunch," I continued. "It's like the school has given us the gift of anorexia."

"All right!" Caroline cheered. "Glass half full." She clinked her can of Diet Coke against mine.

Jamie reached over and snatched the Tater Tots off my tray. "Well, *I* don't want to lose weight," he said. "I'm bulking up. Gonna go out for the football team this year."

"Oh, really?" Abby asked, eyeing Jamie's scrawny arms and chest.

"Hell, yeah!" Jamie said. He pushed up his sleeves and kissed his biceps, flexing the nonexistent muscle. "When Coach sees these cannons, he's gonna make me quarterback."

We all laughed. Then a nasal, saccharine voice broke through our conversation.

"No *way*. This table is *ours*."

I looked up, dreading the sight of the voice's owner.

Sterling Prep has the same annoying social structure as every other high school in America, and Juliet Hammond considers herself Sterling's queen bee. She's beautiful, popular, incredibly nasty, and hands-down my least favorite person in the entire known world.

"Excuse me?" I said.

"That's our table," Juliet repeated. "The Pradas had it saved."

That's another thing. Ever since they saw *Mean Girls*, Juliet and her friends decided their clique needed a name to make them even more elitist and stuck-up. They'd started calling themselves "the Pradas," which was ridiculous in a million ways. Not the least of which was the fact that there was nothing even vaguely Prada-ish about Juliet's Shetland sweater and A-line skirt.

Thankfully, the name hadn't stuck—except with Juliet and her most pathetic hangers-on. The rest of the cliques in school, who remained happily unmonikered, just referred to

Juliet's crowd as "the popular kids" or, more frequently, "those bitches."

But the *most* repulsive thing about Juliet's crowd was that they were all a bunch of enthusiastic, unrepentant, overly spirited *joiners*.

They were the chairs of the homecoming committee, the heads of the cheerleading squad, the captains of the sports teams, and the stars of the school play.

To the faculty and administration, they were the cream of the crop—the pride of the school.

But to us, they were just . . . fake. We protested Juliet and all her ilk by remaining steadfastly and resolutely *anti-join*.

I mean, it's not like we were outcasts or loners. We all got good grades, got along with our teachers, and spent the seven hours we were required to be at Sterling quite happily.

But life *out*side school was so much more interesting than anything *in*side. I didn't really see why I should waste time joining a club in the name of "school spirit."

"You can't save tables," I informed Juliet. "Sit somewhere else."

Juliet narrowed her eyes at me. "Nice outfit, Marit. Where did you get it? Out of the bin at the homeless shelter?"

Juliet's best friend, Emberly, let out a snort. "Don't be mean, Jules," she said. "It's not her fault her father doesn't have a job."

Pop!

My father, for the record, is an artist. He paints huge abstracts that hang in offices and galleries all over the country. He even has one at the MoMA, the Museum of Modern Art in New York. He has his painting studio at home and sets his own hours. But all the way back in elementary school, the girls in Juliet's group decided that since my dad was available to chaperone field trips and volunteer as room parent, it meant he was unemployed. They added that to the ammunition they used to torment me.

When I was younger, I would fly into a rage when they'd insult my dad. And to be honest, it still stung. I was about to let loose with some choice words, but before I could say anything, Jamie jumped in.

"Jeez, Emberly, how do you breathe through that thing?" he asked, staring at her nose.

Emberly Palmer had the distinction of being the youngest person in Connecticut to have gotten cosmetic surgery— a nose job when she was in third grade. Still, she tried to pretend that her face wasn't store-bought and would scream at anyone who suggested otherwise.

"Shut up, loser," she retorted.

Jamie grinned. "Ooh, good one."

Juliet, meanwhile, was getting impatient. She stamped her ballet-flat-clad foot angrily. "Are you freaks going to move or not?" she demanded.

"Not," we all chorused.

She gave us a murderous look, but there was nothing she could do. She flipped us the bird, turned, and stalked over to the other good table to bully the chess club geeks into moving.

Jamie put a hand over his heart. "When we graduate, I'm really gonna *miss* her."

We all laughed, but the smiles faded from our faces when we looked down at the food on our trays. Nine a.m. really *was* a ridiculous time for lunch.

We had calculus next, and the teacher jumped right into the lesson, barely giving us time to get settled at our desks. The board swam with numbers, equations, and formulas.

Don't teachers realize that no one is ready to start learning anything until at least the second day of school?

At least we'd get a break in gym, I thought, but apparently I had underestimated the depths of Ms. Vandermeer's sadism.

Ignoring protests that none of us had our gym clothes, Ms. Vandermeer told us to head out onto the floor and find a partner for "pillow polo," a game that consisted of trying to knock your partner down by whacking her with what looked like a gigantic Q-Tip.

"This is so wrong," Caroline whispered.

"Diabolical," I agreed.

Pop!

The two of us grudgingly stomped out onto the gym floor and picked up our Q-Tips—wooden sticks about six feet long with bright yellow and red padding on the ends.

"Ms. Vandermeer is a monster," Caroline muttered under her breath. "How can she force us to get all sweaty in our clothes? We're going to have to go around stinking all day."

"Um, ever hear of deodorant?" I asked, and whacked her across the butt with my Q-Tip.

"Stop that," Caroline protested. She tried to hit me back, but I blocked her shot with my stick and then got her again across the back of the knees.

"Good shot, Marit!" Ms. Vandermeer shouted from the sidelines. She clapped and gave me a double thumbs-up.

"I hate this," Caroline whined, flinching as I walloped her again.

"You're only saying that because I'm winning," I told her. I pushed a strand of hair out of my face, and Caroline used the break to wave at our teacher.

"Ms. Vandermeer, I can't play. I have cramps."

"Exercise is the best thing for them," Ms. Vandermeer told her. "Now get to it!"

I shot Caroline a what-did-I-tell-you look, but she wasn't paying attention. Swiveling her head around the gym, she caught sight of a girl named Dana.

She was sitting on the bleachers, flipping through an issue

of *Teen People*. This was the first class I'd ever been in with Dana, so I'd never actually spoken to her. I knew who she was, though—everyone did.

Dana had a reputation for being a total skank. I noted this, but since I was completely preoccupied with having sex myself, it seemed wrong to judge.

"How come Dana doesn't have to play?" Caroline asked.

Ms. Vandermeer narrowed her eyes. "That's Dana's business."

"But it's not fair," Caroline argued. "Why does she get to sit out while the rest of us have to play?"

"Dana has a medical reason that excuses her from participation," Ms. Vandermeer said. She turned to signal that the conversation was over, but Caroline wouldn't be deterred.

"I have a medical excuse too," she called out. "I'm . . . delicate."

"Caroline—" Ms. Vandermeer took a warning step toward us, but Dana spoke up from her seat.

"It's fine, Ms. V. Everybody's going to find out sooner or later anyway." Dana turned to Caroline. "I can't play because I'm pregnant."

Everybody froze, trying not to stare.

My mouth dropped open.

Pregnant at seventeen. Jesus. It was like she was the star of her very own Lifetime movie.

And we were complaining about *second-period lunch*?

Dana was still staring at Caroline, waiting for a response.

"Um." Caroline shot me a panicked look, but I had no idea how to help her. "C-congratulations?" she choked out.

There was an awkward pause while everybody tried not to meet anyone else's eyes. Then Mrs. Vandermeer blew her whistle. "All right, girls, let's get back to the game."

Dana buried her face in her magazine, and Caroline and I squared off again.

"I can't believe she's going to have a *baby*," I said, lightly bonking Caroline on the shoulder with my stick.

"Yeah," she answered. "Kind of makes you rethink your whole dying-to-lose-your-virginity thing, huh?"

She planted her Q-Tip in my chest and knocked me to the ground.

I arrived in German class the next period rumpled and reeking. I slumped down in a desk at the very back of the room, already bored. In eighth grade my father had convinced me to sign up for German, and by the time I discovered that only misfits and oddballs studied German, it was too late to switch languages.

Half the kids in my German class were hard-core science geeks who stopped talking to me when I admitted I had never heard of Max Planck. The other half were gloomy goth kids, who never talked much to begin with.

Jamie and Caroline were living it up in Senora Perez's Spanish class, learning to make authentic guacamole and playing Puerto Vallarta Monopoly, while I was stuck doing endless verb declensions in the gulag otherwise known as Herr Robinson's classroom.

The other kids in the class were doing the standard first-day-back catch-up, but since I knew none of them were interested in the art class I'd taken over the summer, I didn't bother to talk to anyone. Instead I concentrated on the top of my desk, where someone had carved, *Foxy Loves Hound.*

Who were these two lovebirds? I wondered. And did Hound love Foxy back?

I traced the grooves with my pencil and let my mind wander. Surprisingly, it wandered back to Dana.

How did anyone let themselves get pregnant in this day and age? I wondered. Didn't she read *Seventeen*? Half the articles in there were about birth control.

Maybe she was too embarrassed to buy condoms?

Man, if I ever managed to find a guy to do it with, you could be sure I wasn't going to let the checkout guy at the Duane Reade screw things up. Dude could get on the mike. Call for a price check for all I cared. Better safe than . . . well, Dana.

I was so preoccupied with this train of thought that I didn't bother to look up when Herr Robinson cleared his throat.

"Okay, *Klassen*," he said, speaking in his annoying mix of German and English. "We have a new student joining us *heute*. Let's all *sagan Wilkommen* to Noah Bailey."

Someone new? I glanced up to gaze upon the sad soul who'd chosen German for his language requirement—and froze.

There, standing in a bright beam of sunlight, was the most amazing guy I had ever seen.

He had longish brown hair, and his eyes were bright, even from here. He stood at the front of the classroom, completely at ease. A smile flickered across his face. It was the most open, brilliant smile in the entire universe.

If I had been standing up, my knees would have buckled. As it was, I swooned into the back of my desk.

The rest of the class murmured, "*Wilkommen*, Noah," while I took in the view. This guy was *gorgeous*. And he took *German*!

I flashed Noah a big smile, but he sank down into the empty seat closest to the door.

Damn. If I had any hope of getting to him before the rest of the twelfth-grade hyenas—I mean, girls—I'd have to talk to him. And to do that? I needed to *sit next to him*.

Biggest problem? Getting up and changing my seat. It seemed so *obvious*. I needed a good excuse or, barring that, the courage to act without explanation.

To *be* obvious.

Ms. Vandermeer was always shouting slogans at us to rev us up in gym—why hadn't I paid more attention last period?

I racked my brain for some properly motivational material.

"Be all that you can be"?

Didn't really fit the situation.

"Go for it"?

Too blah.

Finally I decided on the Lotto motto: "You gotta be in it to win it."

Yeah. That'd do.

I murmured it to myself as I scooped up my books and sauntered toward the desk next to Noah's.

"Better acoustics on this side of the room," I told him breezily, and slipped into the seat next to his.

Noah turned to face me, and my heart skipped about a million beats. Up close, he was even hotter than I'd realized. His hair was a bit long, but not in a pretentious or girly way—just like he was too busy being adorable to get it cut. And his eyes weren't so much brown as the color of gravel—brownish gray. He had a smattering of freckles across the bridge of his nose, and I had to fight the urge to lick them.

Well, not really, but they *were* awfully cute.

He met my gaze, and his lips curled into a lazy smile.

"Hey," he said in a soft voice. He reached his hand out to touch my hair.

Whoa! That Lotto motto is *effective!* I thought. I felt a flutter in my chest.

Then Noah pulled his hand back, grasping a piece of bright yellow foam.

Blood rushed to my face as I realized what it was—a tiny piece of the giant Q-Tip from gym class!

Oh my God. I just left there! I was sweaty and smelly, and now apparently it looked like I'd been rolling around on the floor!

I was about to add my curses to Caroline's at the injustice of middle-of-the-day gym. Then I realized that Noah was still looking at me. And *smiling.*

I needed to say something—anything—but my mind was a complete blank.

Say hi! Just say hi, my brain commanded, but my lips wouldn't form the word.

Instead I opened my mouth and closed it a few times, while my face grew redder and redder.

They say you only get one chance to make a first impression. Well, with each second that passed, my first impression was looking more and more like "giant tuna in a D cup."

Noah's expression grew concerned. Like he suddenly

realized he'd taken a seat next to the school's only main-streamed developmentally disabled girl, and now he was going to have to be nice to her and keep her from eating the paste.

The situation was critical—I could see my future as the world's oldest living virgin stretching out ahead of me—so I gave myself a pinch on the leg to jolt myself from my trance.

"HI!!!" I ended up shouting, so loudly that the entire class jumped.

God, what was *wrong* with me?

"I mean, *hi*," I said in a normal volume. "Sorry—I've been listening to my iPod all day. Messes with your hearing."

Okay, that didn't sound especially crazy. Of course, it didn't sound especially *bright*. . . .

But at least Noah stopped looking frightened. After a second he smiled back at me.

"Ich heiss Noah. Wie heisen Sie?"

"Ich heiss Marit. Wie geht's?" I answered, pretty much exhausting my entire German vocabulary. "You're new, right?" I added.

"Yeah," Noah said. "We just moved here from Texas a couple of weeks ago." He leaned back in his chair and stretched. His T-shirt rode up a little way on his stomach, revealing—gulp!—six-pack abs.

I forced my eyes back up to his face before I started drooling.

Pop!

"It must suck having to switch schools senior year," I said, but Noah shrugged.

"I don't know." He looked me up and down. "Some of it's not so bad."

I felt my face flush warm. Was he talking about *me*? I had to keep my wits about me—play it cool.

"Yeah?" I drawled, narrowing my eyes to seductive slits.

"Yeah. You know, I like living this close to New York City," he said, "and it'll be cool to be here this winter, 'cause I ski."

Down, girl, I scolded myself. *He wasn't talking about you. Which means he doesn't want you. Yet.*

"There's cool stuff to do around here all year long," I told him. "And my friends and I go into the city practically every weekend if you ever, uh, need suggestions about where to go."

Noah's smile faded, and I mentally kicked myself. Why didn't I just invite him to come with us?

Hold on—maybe it wasn't too late.

I opened my mouth, but before I could get out another word, Herr Robinson rapped on his desk to get the class's attention.

As our teacher droned on about the first week's vocabulary lists, I watched Noah out of the corner of my eye.

If I invite him to come into the city with Caroline, Jamie, and me, it might sound friend-like, I thought. *And I have plenty of friends already.*

Maybe I should figure out somewhere else to take him. Somewhere more . . . date-y.

And just like that, it hit me. Of course! The back-to-school bonfire!

Every year Sterling had a big party on the beach to get everyone revved up for the new school year. It was a little too rah-rah for my tastes—Jamie, Caroline, and I planned to go solely in an ironic capacity. . . .

But the waves, the fire, the moonlight . . . it could be romantic.

To say nothing of the fact that I'd get to see Noah in a bathing suit.

The bonfire was this Friday night, so I needed to act fast.

Noah was paying attention to Herr Robinson, who was wandering up and down the aisles of the classroom, pronouncing each vocabulary word for us.

"Der Bahnhof," he droned.

"Der Bahnhof," Noah repeated.

"Die Fahrkarte."

"Die Fahrkarte."

I didn't repeat the words with the rest of the class. Instead I ripped a piece of paper out of my notebook.

I chewed on the end of my pencil and tried to come up with a clever way to invite Noah to the bonfire. I wanted to find just the right words—

Pop!

Things will really heat up this Friday. . . .
You're hot, and so is the bonfire. . . .
Sparks are flying. . . .

Ugh. Why not just *beg* him to turn me down?

A half an hour later the bell was about to ring, so finally I just scrawled, *You. Me. Bonfire. Friday. Yes?*

I read it over. Not bad. Straightforward. Sexy.

All right—let's do this.

I folded the note into a tiny little cube and flicked it onto Noah's desk. He scooped it into his palm and opened it. He read the note, then scrawled something at the bottom. But before he could pass it back to me, Herr Robinson intercepted it, plucking the note off Noah's desk and dropping it into the wastebasket without missing a beat.

"Das Flugzeug," Herr Robinson droned.

Noah shot me a guilty glance out of the corner of his eye.

"Das Flugzeug," I mumbled, silently willing him to nod or shake his head or do *anything* to let me know his answer.

The bell rang a minute later. Noah grabbed his books and dashed off after Herr Robinson, who was clutching an empty coffee mug and booking it toward the teachers' lounge.

I hung my head low.

I'm repellant, I thought. *I'm human Deet.* Why else would Noah run away?

I lingered at my desk until the last German student left,

then surrendered the last shreds of my dignity as I scrabbled through the trash can, looking for the note.

I finally spotted it lying next to someone's spit-out bubble gum. I grimaced and gingerly picked it up, smoothing it out on the desk.

I held my breath and looked at what he'd written.

YES

?

!!!

Oh my God. This is it, I told myself as I carefully tucked the note into a pocket of my backpack. Fresh start! New beginning! Second chance to make a first impression!

I slung my backpack over my shoulder and headed down the hall toward English class.

I won't ruin this relationship, I told myself. *No way.*

I was going to date Noah, and hook up with him, and maybe even have sex with him at some point down the line—and I was going to do it all without freaking out or getting scared or blowing it in some other humiliating way.

In a word, the bonfire was going to be . . . awesome.

I got to English class and slipped into the seat Jamie had saved for me.

I could feel it, a buzzing that started in my stomach and tingled its way along my spine.

This time, I vowed, it was all going to be *perfect.*

Pop!

"Hey, Marit," Jamie said, "you've got something stuck in your hair."

He reached out and grabbed a bright red piece of foam from my curls.

I closed my eyes for a moment. Gathered myself.

Yes. It was all going to be perfect, I thought.

Starting right . . . *now*.

4

Friday morning I woke up at the crack of dawn. I was so excited about my evening with Noah that I had barely slept. I jumped in the shower—even though I'd be showering again after gym—then threw on my clothes and skipped down the stairs.

Early as it was, I found Caroline seated at the kitchen table. My dad was cooking her breakfast.

My father is always happy to have Caroline around. She's another mouth to feed, and cooking is his favorite way to relax. At least, when he isn't painting.

"How many strips of bacon would you girls like?" he asked, kissing me on the cheek as he simultaneously stirred the eggs and pulled a block of Parmesan out of the fridge.

"Three, please," I answered, grabbing a glass from the

cupboard and pouring myself some orange juice. I gulped down half of it in one swallow, then carried it over to the table.

"And for you, Caro-bean?" Dad asked.

"None, thank you," Caroline answered. "I'll just have some yogurt or something."

My dad and I both froze. Caroline had been known to put away eight or nine slices of bacon at a sitting. Her refusal of pork products was a sure sign that something was not right in the universe.

"Excuse me?" my dad asked, the refrigerator door hanging open. "Are you feeling okay?"

He walked over to her and placed his palm on her forehead, concerned.

"I'm fine. I've just decided to become a vegetarian," Caroline said, spreading jam on a piece of toast.

I snorted, and some OJ came up through my nose. It stung like crazy, and I coughed into a napkin as tears streamed down my cheeks.

My dad checked to make sure I wasn't dying, then turned to Caroline, amused. "So, Miss Caroline, what brought about this sudden spate of health and social consciousness?"

"Meat is murder, Mr. Anders," Caroline said matter-of-factly. "From now on, I'm not eating anything with a face."

"Nothing with a face," Dad said. "Well, I can certainly respect that. One yogurt coming up."

He turned his back to us and spent a moment at the counter, humming as he prepared our breakfasts. After a minute he came back to the table and put a plate down in front of each of us.

Mine had the standard eggs-bacon-muffin that I ate more days than not.

Caroline's plate, however, was something else.

In the middle of a perfectly round puddle of vanilla yogurt, my dad had used raisins, almonds, and slices of fresh fruit to construct a mosaic face, which smiled up at us.

It was a masterpiece, really too beautiful to eat, and Caroline stared at it, her mouth hanging open.

Dad smiled at her, a challenge. "What are you going to do about that, Caro-bean?"

She shrugged and reached for my bacon. "Well, if I'm eating faces anyway," she said, and shoved a piece in her mouth.

"Hey!" I protested.

But my dad laughed and hugged her. The way Caroline's face lit up made me not even begrudge her my breakfast.

Dad turned back to the stove to put a couple more slices of bacon on the griddle, and Caroline leaned back in her chair, helping herself to the last slice on my plate.

"So, do you know what you're going to wear to the bonfire tonight?" she asked.

When I told Caroline and Jamie about Noah, they seemed

a little doubtful that I could break out of my old pattern. But since I was determined that this time things would be different, they promised to do whatever they could to help.

The first step, Caroline instructed, was to wear something for our date that would make me look hot.

"I was thinking my vintage terry-cloth halter dress. You know, the one straight out of the seventies," I said. "Cute, right?"

"You'll freeze." Caroline shook her head. "It's supposed to get down to sixty tonight."

That was the problem with Connecticut. It was only warm enough to go swimming two months of the year.

"Then I don't have a single thing to wear," I complained.

"I'd lend you something of mine," Caroline offered, "but I think your girls would stretch it out of shape." She pointed first at her boobs, then at mine.

"Caroline!" I laughed.

"Maybe Hilly has something you can borrow."

I shot her a glance, warning her to shut up, but she didn't notice.

"Her Roxy outfit is cute and wouldn't be out of place at the bonfire—"

"I'll find something in my closet, I'm sure," I said quickly.

My dad raised an eyebrow. "You don't have to be afraid to say your sister's name, you know."

Sure, I didn't have to be afraid. As long as I didn't mind a lot of shouting and slammed doors.

"Matter of fact, she should join us for breakfast," Dad said. "Enough sulking in her room. We'll all eat together. *Like a family.*"

He marched determinedly out of the room.

I winced. Screaming and slamming doors in T-minus 10, 9, 8 . . .

Caroline shot me a guilty look. "Sorry. How's she doing, anyway?"

I rolled my eyes. "My parents want to take her up to Massachusetts in a couple of weeks to check out colleges, but for now she says she's not going."

"Poor Hilly," Caroline sympathized.

"Yeah, it's all a little . . . tense around here."

"Then let's think about other things," she said through a mouthful of bacon. "Like you and Noah *doing it!*"

"Shhh!" I looked over my shoulder to make sure my dad wasn't on his way back. "It's not like we're going to do it right away. I'm going to wait until I'm sure that he really loves and respects me—"

"I don't know," she said with a wicked grin. "Maybe you should hurry up and get it over with before you turn into a basket case and break up with him."

"Right." I smirked at her. "Forget love and respect—I'm jumping him tonight!"

Caroline and I both cracked up.

"Oh, Noah," she simpered in a high-pitched voice that was supposed to be mine, "I want you so bad. Won't you turn this girl into a woman?"

"Shut up!" I laughed.

"But I have *needs*, Noah. Needs that only you can satisfy."

"Caroline!"

She grabbed me by the arms and fluttered her eyelashes dramatically. "Take me, Noah. I'm a—a ripe peach, waiting to be . . . *plucked*. . . ."

The room echoed with her cackles.

"Stop," I said, giving her a shove. "My dad's going to hear you!"

"What am I going to hear?" my dad asked, walking back into the kitchen.

I made a face at Caroline. *Told you so!*

Caroline cleared her throat. "I was just saying that it's a shame you raised such a piggy little daughter who ate all the bacon and left none for the rest of us."

"I've had one piece!" I said. "You're the one who scarfed it all down."

"Yet I want more," she said.

Dad reached into the refrigerator and pulled out the slab of bacon. "Anything for our vegetarian friends."

Caroline gave me a wink, then reached for my glass of orange juice.

I shook my head at her.

Obviously I wasn't going to sleep with Noah on our very first date, but since I planned to somewhere down the line, tonight was about setting the sex wheels in motion.

I was going to mack on Noah till my lips were sore. And no matter what, I was not going to get scared and run away.

I was unleashing the new, confident, sexy me.

And if things happened to get a little more physical than I was used to? Well, *good.*

5

We ain't bad, and we ain't cocky! Gonna ride on you like a Kawasaki!"

The Sterling cheer squad pranced up and down the sand in front of the bonfire, twisting their hands like they were revving motorcycles.

"Vroom, vroom! Go, go, go! We're gonna beat you, lay you low."

Noah vroomed his hands too, cheering along with the other students who weren't embarrassed about showing school spirit: the Pradas, their boyfriends, athletes, student council members, and, not astoundingly, Jamie and Caroline, who believed you couldn't truly mock something unless you had first experienced it on a visceral level.

I stood next to Noah, clapping along halfheartedly.

Normally I wouldn't have been caught dead anywhere near the cheer squad, even for the sake of being ironic. But the promise of hooking up with Noah was worth looking like the sort of person in whose hands pom-poms would not be out of place.

Hooking up, however, appeared to be the last thing on Noah's mind. The minute we got to the beach, he threw himself into the occasion with a peppiness usually reserved for kids running for class president. He helped gather driftwood for the fire and tossed a Frisbee around with a couple of freshmen. He even took his turn at the grill, flipping burgers. He shook hands with the principal, hit a double in the softball game, and in general was so friendly and gung ho I half expected the football team to hoist him on their shoulders and parade him down the beach.

Normally? *Gag.*

But then Noah glanced over at me, and the sparks from the bonfire brought out golden flecks in his eyes.

Opposite of *gag.*

The cheer ended. Noah put his arm around my shoulders, giving me a little squeeze.

"Is your pep not being rallied?" he asked. "'Cause if you got spirit, I don't hear it."

"We aren't even playing another team!" I complained. "Who or what are we supposed to be getting riled up about?"

Noah shrugged. "Guess you have your choice. I, personally, am gonna use my screech owl power against the tyranny of second-period lunch!"

I laughed, and his smile grew wider. "Hey, I saw a couple of watermelons on the picnic table. I told Mrs. Kent I'd carve them up for her. Wanna help?"

I resisted the urge to roll my eyes.

"Uh, I think I'm going to go talk to Caroline for a minute," I said.

"Okay. Be right back." Noah gave my shoulder one last squeeze before walking away.

I wandered over to my friends.

"Having fun?" Jamie asked as I came up.

I shrugged. "At least I don't have to worry about things getting too physical. At this rate I'll have graduated college before I get a second alone with him."

"Where is he?" Caroline asked, looking around.

I scowled. "He's off earning his merit badge in snack preparation."

Caroline smiled sympathetically. "You must really be crazy about him if you still want to be alone with him after that display."

I gave them a pleading look. "It's not *that* bad, is it? I mean, you guys thought he was cool and all, right?"

"Definitely," Caroline said, but I could see her struggling not to smirk.

"He's, ummm, peppy," Jamie said. "You gotta give him that."

My shoulders slumped. "You guys, I really like him. Even with all his ridiculous school spirit. He's not like the other kids. He seems . . . genuine, you know? I want it to work out."

"It will," Jamie said. "He's just acting all involved because he's new and wants to meet people. Deep down, I bet he's as cynical and apathetic as the rest of us."

I folded my hands and looked up to heaven. "We can only hope."

Caroline glanced over my shoulder, troubled. "Oh God, look who he's talking to now."

I turned, and my heart sank. Noah was standing next to Rick Fielding, laughing at something he'd said.

Rick was the biggest jerk in school—the star of the lacrosse team and Juliet Hammond's boyfriend.

He was a juiced-up meathead who never missed an opportunity to beat someone up, or key their car, or find some other way to make them miserable.

Jamie *especially* hated him. In fifth grade Rick smashed the model of Pompeii Jamie had spent weeks making for social studies. Jamie burst into tears as he looked down at the devastation, and Rick told everyone in class that Jamie was a crybaby.

Rick never missed an opportunity to rag on Jamie after

that. Which made Jamie's main objective at Sterling finding new ways to avoid Rick.

Translation: If Noah made friends with Rick Fielding, there was no way I could ever date him. And since there were no other viable dating options at Sterling, I might as well get fitted for a chastity belt.

"Oh no," I breathed. "What should I do? Should I go over there?"

But Noah glanced over and caught me looking at him. He said something to Rick, then headed my way.

"There you are," he said, including Jamie and Caroline in his smile.

"What were you—I mean, how do you know Rick Fielding?" I asked him, struggling to keep my voice casual.

"I just met him over by the watermelons," Noah said.

Jamie, Caroline, and I let out big sighs of relief.

"Nice guy," Noah continued cautiously. "He told me about this spot down the beach where you can't see any of the light from town. The stars are supposed to be amazing."

"Meyer's Rocks," I said, trying to ignore the poke Caroline gave me in the small of my back.

Meyer's Rocks was the biggest make-out spot in all of Greenwich. I'd never been there on a date, but when Jamie got his driver's license, the three of us drove out there once. You really could see the stars. . . .

"You, uh, maybe want to check it out?" Noah asked.

Caroline poked me again.

"S-sure," I said, shooting a glance at my friends.

Noah wrapped his large, warm hand around mine, and we started down the beach, away from the noisy throng of students clustered around the bonfire.

"Have fun," Caroline called after us.

"And Marit," Jamie chimed in, "be good!"

Noah and I walked until the shoreline curved and we were out of sight of the fire. We could see dark shapes in the sand—other kids looking for privacy—and heard the occasional giggle or sigh that let me know I wasn't the only one with dirty deeds on the brain.

Finally we passed even those people and were completely, blissfully alone. Meyer's Rocks was a couple hundred yards farther down the beach. It was a cluster of giant, smooth boulders half buried in the sand above the crashing surf. Noah led me over to one of the rocks. He scrambled to the top of it, then turned and held out a hand to help me up.

I hesitated.

Admit the problem and the problem will go away, I reminded myself. *Okay. Problem: I tend to get freaky when things get physical, but I don't have to do anything I don't want. If we're moving too fast, I can just slow down—or stop—without acting like a loon.*

Pop!

"You coming?" Noah asked in a low, sweet voice. I nodded and took his hand.

We lay back on the rock, looking up at the dazzling display of stars in the sky.

Suddenly I found it hard to breathe.

I could picture my entire glorious senior year with Noah as my boyfriend. Holding hands as we walked to class, leaving notes in each other's lockers. He'd tell me he loved me, and I'd say it back. It would be the sort of romance I'd always dreamed about but never actually experienced.

We'd be Romeo and Juliet . . . without all the inconvenient suicide. And it was starting right here, right now.

Noah turned his gaze from the sky to my face. He gave me a small, secret smile.

"Gorgeous," he said softly.

"Yeah, you really can see the stars out here," I said, amazed at my Oscar-worthy portrayal of calmness.

"I wasn't talking about the stars," he murmured.

My breath caught in my throat. Noah brought his lips to mine, and it was hands down the best kiss of my life. A kiss that would fuel a decade's worth of fantasies.

Noah closed his eyes and totally gave in to the moment.

I wrapped my arms around his neck as he continued to kiss me—softly, then gradually, more urgently. We sank back onto the rock, so that he was half lying on top of me. He moved his hands through my hair, over my back, lightly stroking the bare skin of my shoulders.

His fingers slipped beneath the neckline of my dress, trailing along my collarbone.

My heartbeat sped up, as much from excitement as from sheer nervousness.

I quickly took stock and decided, no, I wasn't scared, and yes, I wanted more.

I moved my lips to his neck, breathing in his warm boy smell, kissing the spot where his neck and shoulder met. He shuddered a little as my lips brushed his skin.

Noah pulled me closer with one arm while his other hand moseyed its way around to my front.

Oh my God. Were we moving too fast?

I wanted Noah to keep going, but I didn't want him to think I was slutty.

I made an executive decision: the boob was fine, but anything lower was Skank City. I wouldn't move his hand away unless . . .

He moved it himself.

Why did he move it himself?

Noah propped himself up on one arm and grinned at me. "How you doing?"

"I'm great," I said. Then, "Why'd you stop?"

Noah's grin grew wider. "Just wanted to check in. Make sure we weren't going too fast."

Oh my God, it was like he could read my mind. I pulled his head back down to mine.

We kissed again, and Noah's hand snaked under the bottom of my shirt. I could hear my pulse pounding in my ears. Could feel little beads of sweat forming just above my eyebrows.

My whole body flushed.

Suddenly I was overly warm. I needed a little space. I needed air.

I needed it *now.*

I shifted my weight, trying to find a different position on the boulder. An instant too late I realized how close I was to the edge.

I tried to shift my body back the other way, but I lost my balance and started to slip.

"Whoa!" I shouted. The next thing I knew, I was falling!

I flailed my arms, trying to find a handhold, grabbing wildly for something to hold on to. My fingers brushed against fabric, and I clutched at it, thinking that if I held on to Noah's shirt, I could stop myself from falling.

One hand grabbed onto the pocket of Noah's polo, but the other . . . the other wasn't holding his shirt at all.

It was clutching his jeans.

More specifically, the *front* of his jeans.

Most specifically, the part of his body that was *inside* the front of his jeans!

Holy crap! I snatched my hand away and started tumbling off the rock again.

Noah grabbed me by the shoulders and kept me from hitting the sand.

The second I was steady, I scrambled away from him.

God! I was so embarrassed I thought I would spontaneously combust—looked forward to it, actually.

"Okay, *that's* going too fast," Noah joked, but I didn't see anything funny about it.

I choked out a "Sorry!," then turned and ran away up the beach.

I could hear Noah calling after me, but I didn't stop. I ran as fast as I could and never once looked back.

6

The house was mercifully empty when I got home. My parents were at a benefit, and Hilly was maintaining her self-imposed exile in her room.

I threw my purse down as I walked in the door and kicked off my shoes.

I stomped into the kitchen, praying that there was ice cream in the freezer. Salvation—most of a pint of Phish Food left.

I grabbed the carton, marched into the living room, and flipped on the TV.

MTV *Cribs* was on, but I couldn't pay attention to the details of Bow Wow's pool house. I was too preoccupied with the fact that my social life at Sterling was officially over.

I couldn't believe the way I had humiliated myself. I really *was* frigid. And a loser.

A frigid, penis-grabbing loser with zero chance of having a real relationship. I was ruined! I'd have to transfer to an all-girls school! Because clearly, guys and me? Not working out.

I spooned a gigantic glob of ice cream into my mouth and winced.

Ow! Brain freeze.

Did life ever *stop* sucking?

I flipped through the channels and squeezed the sides of the Phish Food carton, willing the ice cream to soften.

What if something really was wrong with me? Like, unless I got massive psychological help, I'd *never* live a happy and fulfilling life. . . .

Marit, interrupted.

I sighed. This was totally pointless. Maybe I could find another way to take my mind off my troubles.

I shut off the TV and went upstairs. I dragged my boom box into the bathroom with me and put on my Strokes CD. I turned it up as loud as it would go and got into the shower. It was home spa time.

I picked up Hilly's pomegranate shampoo and, even though I knew she would kill me, poured out a huge handful.

"Is this it? Is this it?" I sang along, scowling. The scalding water pummeled me, raising red splotches on my skin.

I used Hilly's matching body scrub and shower gel in an attempt to slough off the entire evening. I stayed sudsy until the CD ended. Then I turned off the shower and pressed down the stopper so the water started to fill the bath.

I reached out and, terrified of being electrocuted, carefully hit the play button. The CD started again, and I sank down in the bath.

I lay there, staring at the lime green tiles. As hard as I tried, I couldn't get Noah out of my mind.

As much as I wanted to forget my humiliation, I kept remembering all the stuff that had happened *before* I slipped off the rock.

The warmth of Noah's hands on my skin. The way his hair smelled like wood smoke and sunshine. The feel of his lips on mine.

I cast my mind back to that moment. My blood raced at the thought of it. I closed my eyes and could *feel* it.

Lips, hands, his breath on my neck—

I grew dizzy.

I put my feet up on either side of the faucet and slid down so the water was hitting me in just the right spot. I'd read about this once, in a book Hilly gave me. "Page one fifty-six," she'd whispered, giggling.

I never did thank her.

I shut my eyes and remembered the way Noah's body felt pressed against mine. I lowered myself so that my ears were underwater, the music from my CD distorted.

I couldn't hear the lyrics, just the beat, the pulse of the song cascading over me.

As the water in the tub rose, a wave built up inside me. The music thumped so loudly that my heart picked up its rhythm, beating along in time to the drums.

Images of Noah flashed through my brain—his eyes, his hands, his body shivering with pleasure.

I imagined how things *could* have gone. Feeling his skin . . . his muscles tight . . . the way he whispered my name . . .

"Noah," I said softly—and as the water in the tub threatened to pour over the sides, the wave inside me came crashing down.

I turned off the water. Not a second too soon.

The Strokes were still singing, but I lowered the volume all the way down as I toweled off and got into my pajamas.

Around ten and unable to sleep, I finally padded down the hall to Hilly's room. My sister was no stranger to tragedy—or to sex. She and her boyfriend, Thad, had had plenty of both in the last three years, so maybe she'd have some advice. I knocked on her door and waited.

Hilly opened the door a crack and peered out, scowling. When she saw that it was me and not my parents standing in the hall, her face relaxed.

"Come," she said. She retreated into her room and flopped down on her bed, where she'd apparently been hard at work braiding her hair into little Björk-style knots.

I followed her in, peering cautiously around.

Hilly used to have a bunch of Georgetown posters up on her walls, but when they rejected her, she ripped them all down.

In the last few weeks, it appeared, she'd redecorated.

The room was now wallpapered with pictures of her friends. She'd replaced her desk chair with one of those weird kneely computer chairs, and she'd cleared away her zillions of stuffed animals and knickknacks, replacing them with piles and piles of books.

I picked a few of them up and read the titles. *Aristophanes' Collected Plays. Practical Spoken Russian. Gray's Anatomy. Jung Made Simple.*

Weird.

"What's up with the library?" I asked.

"I'm becoming an autodidact," she said. "Just because Georgetown thinks I'm stupid doesn't mean I have to prove them right."

I didn't bother arguing with her. No matter how hard we tried to convince Hilly that Georgetown wasn't personally out to ruin her life, she refused to listen. Not even Noah, with his insane peppiness, would be able to lift my sister's spirits on *that* topic.

Oh God . . . *Noah.*

I sank down onto the foot of Hilly's bed with a moan.

She frowned. "What's wrong? And why are you home so early? I thought the bonfire didn't end until eleven."

"I can't ever go back there," I said. For the first time in the entire evening, a tear escaped from my eye. "I made such a fool of myself."

Hilly threw her arms around me. "Oh, honey. What happened? Is there someone I need to beat up?"

I gave a little smile. Even though she was miserable for her own reasons, I'd known that Hilly would be there for me.

"There's this new boy in school. Noah," I started. "He's so cute—"

Hilly nodded, reaching for the bowl of Pringles on her nightstand.

"Tonight we were kissing. And I accidentally grabbed his"—I paused—"*you know.*"

Hilly's eyebrows shot straight up.

"It was completely mortifying," I finished.

Hilly regarded me silently. "You grabbed his penis . . . *accidentally?*"

I nodded.

"But how did you—"

"Don't make me relive it," I interrupted. "The point is, now he's not going to want to go out with me, and I'll be alone *forever.*"

Hilly offered me the bowl of chips. I shook my head. "Marit. You'll find someone," she tried to reassure me.

"No, I won't," I told her. "There's something wrong with me. Anytime I meet someone I like, I start freaking out about sex, and then I jinx it."

"Whoa, whoa, whoa." Hilly locked eyes with me. "Marit, is

someone pressuring you? If you're not ready to have sex, just tell the guy no. If he gets pissed off, he's a complete cretin and you wouldn't want to date him anyway."

"That's not it," I wailed. "I *am* ready. It's just—the minute things get physical, I start acting like an ass! I spaz out. I sweat. I can't breathe."

I paused for a moment, gathering myself.

"I feel like maybe I'm thinking about it too much, and I don't know how to stop. I think that if I could get it over with . . . if I could just do it *one time*, I wouldn't be weird about it anymore."

Hilly looked at me, considering. "You want to have sex so you don't have to worry about having sex. Right?"

I let out a sigh of relief. I'm so glad she's my sister. "Right."

Hilly popped a chip into her mouth. "What you need," she said, "is a friend-with-benefits."

I opened my mouth, but she held up a hand. "I'm serious. You need to find somebody you get along with, who you're not interested in romantically, that you can just have sex with."

I frowned. "I don't know anybody like that."

Hilly was about to answer when we heard the squeak of the back gate.

My parents got mad if any of our friends rang the doorbell after ten o'clock. So Hilly's and my friends started coming in the back way at night.

Hilly looked out the window. "Be right down!" she called.

I figured it was Thad, but when she turned back to me, she had a funny look on her face. "Okay, I don't want to come across all Tom-and-Elena . . ."

I grinned. It drove my parents crazy that ever since she graduated, Hilly had been calling them by their first names.

". . . but you guys are going to use a condom, right?"

"Who?" I asked, confused.

"You and Jamie."

"*What?*" I yelped.

"Jamie," she repeated. "He's your perfect friend-with-benefits. And he's downstairs right now."

I couldn't help it. I laughed. The whole idea was . . . ridiculous.

Hilly frowned. "Marit. Safe sex is no joke."

"Wait a minute," I said, "you're talking about *Jamie* here."

"I know. And if you *really* think you're ready to have sex, and you *really* just want to get it over with, then Jamie is the perfect choice." She started ticking the reasons off on her fingers. "You really like him as a person. You know he'll be nice to you and treat you well. He's presumably disease free. He's pretty cute. He's available, and most of all, he's *here*."

"Yeah, but"—I tried to find the words to explain how insane her idea was—"but it's *Jamie*."

Hilly grinned and held her bedroom door open. "I know," she said. "Now go get him!"

I walked downstairs and opened the kitchen door to let Jamie in.

"Marit, are you okay?" he asked before he even crossed the threshold. "Noah came back to the bonfire without you. I wanted to make sure you were all right."

I nodded. "I'm fine. I just—hate pep rallies."

"Well, of course you do," Jamie said. "You have a brain."

I sent him a psychic thank-you for not asking what happened with Noah. Instead he reached into his backpack and pulled out a DVD case.

"You left before I could give you that Iranian comedy I told you about last week." He paused. "Maybe you wanna . . ."

He shook the case, grinned at me hopefully.

I rolled my eyes. "You want to watch it now?" I asked, humoring him.

"If you insist," Jamie said. He headed toward the living room.

I followed him slowly, thinking about what Hilly had said.

It was weird—we'd been friends for so long that I never really *saw* Jamie anymore.

I was surprised at how nice his eyes were—a really stormy dark blue. And his lips were definitely sexy—full and pouty, like in paintings of Cupid.

But—he was also an inch shorter than me, probably ten pounds lighter; plus, as I mentioned, I really wasn't a fan of the red hair. . . .

"What?" Jamie asked, looking up from the DVD player and seeing me staring at him.

I shook away my ridiculous thoughts.

"Nothing," I said. "Absolutely, positively nothing."

We sprawled out on the couch to watch the movie, me leaning against him, snuggled up against each other the same as we've done practically every other night of our lives.

Only this time, it felt different.

I never noticed before how heavy and comforting his arm was around my shoulders. It made me feel . . . safe. His skin was warm, and I could feel the heat from his body through his T-shirt.

He wasn't *that* much shorter than I was, I realized. And he also smelled good, like laundry detergent and shampoo and cherry soda.

For the first time since I'd known him, Jamie seemed like a *boy* to me—a boy with potential, a boy I would maybe consider going all the way with.

It completely freaked me out.

I shifted my weight, and Jamie let go of me.

"Want something to drink?" I asked, jumping up.

"I'm good," he answered. He paused the movie so I

73

wouldn't miss any of it, even though I wasn't really paying attention to begin with.

I went into the kitchen and leaned against the refrigerator.

Maybe Hilly was right. Maybe she had given me a simple solution to an otherwise overwhelming problem. Maybe Jamie *could* be my first.

Now all I had to do now was convince him that I should be *his*.

8

I didn't think I'd be able to fall asleep that night. Every time I'd start to drift off, I'd imagine me and Jamie together and jolt awake again.

You could say it was a nightmare, only the more I thought about it, the less scary it seemed.

And the less scary it seemed, the more it started to make sense.

If only I could figure out how to broach the subject with him.

You can't just walk up to a guy and say, "Hey, wanna do it?" Even if he *is* your best friend.

I tossed and turned until the sky outside my windows started to brighten.

Then, a blink later, the sun was high in the clouds. The

clock on my nightstand said eleven, and I could hear Caroline's laughter coming from the kitchen.

Aha! *Caroline* would know what to do.

I jumped out of bed and ran downstairs, where I found her at the kitchen table, eating pancakes and amusing my father with her imitation of the cheerleaders at the bonfire last night.

"Come with me right now," I commanded, grabbing her sleeve and giving it a yank.

Caroline paused, a forkful of pancake frozen halfway to her mouth, dripping syrup on the front of her shirt. She looked at me and her eyes widened, aware that I had Something Big to tell her.

She dropped her fork with a clatter and scraped her chair back from the table.

"So I guess you'll finish your story later?" my dad called after us.

"You bet, Mr. A.," she shouted.

We zipped back up the stairs, tumbled into my room, and slammed the door shut behind us.

I took a deep breath, ready to tell her my new plan, but she jumped in before I could start.

"Oh my God, did you do it?"

I paused, thrown. "Do what?"

Caroline shook her head impatiently. "Did you have sex?"

"With Jamie?" I asked, confused.

Caroline looked at me like I was out of my mind. "What are you talking about? With Noah!"

Oh.

I'd been so fixated on Hilly's idea that I'd forgotten. Caroline hadn't heard about the bonfire.

"Uh, that's hit a snag," I told her.

Caroline threw up her hands, exasperated. "Marit, tell me what happened!"

I knew she wouldn't let me get my news about Jamie out until I filled her in on the whole crotch-grabbing incident. So I relived every painful detail, then shushed her follow-up questions.

"So, last night Hilly had an idea," I said. "I'm freaked out about sex, right?"

"Duh," she responded.

"And I'm not going to stop being freaked out until I do it, right?"

"Right. But you can't find anyone to do it with because you're so freaked out about the thought of doing it in the first place." Caroline shook her head sadly. "The classic chicken-and-egg scenario."

"But there is *one* person who doesn't scare me. And I think . . . I think I should do it with *him*."

"Really?" Caroline stared at me blankly. "Who?"

I took another deep breath, then blurted it out.

"Jamie."

Caroline's mouth fell open. She stared at me, frozen, for so long I thought that maybe she'd had a stroke.

But then she let out a shriek and threw her arms around me. "Oh my God. Oh my *God*! That's *perfect*!"

I grinned, relieved. "It's a good idea, right? 'Cause when Hilly said it, it seemed like maybe that could solve all my problems."

"Are you kidding? I can't believe I never thought of it myself. Oh my God, *you're going to do it with Jamie*!" She let out another shriek and hugged me, laughing.

"Hold on," I told her. "I haven't asked him yet, so I don't know if he'll even be into the idea. . . ."

"Are you kidding?" Caroline said. "He'll be into it. Definitely."

I sat down on my bed and grinned, the idea starting to become real in my mind. "How do you think I should ask him?"

"You could hire a Kyrgyzstani filmmaker to shoot a video," she suggested. "Jamie told me once that was the way he planned to propose . . . if he ever decided to get married."

"Okay," I said. "any ideas that don't involve me traveling to a war zone?"

Caroline thought for a moment. "Lots of guys respond to flattery. Tell him, like, what a stud he is and how your loins are burning for him and stuff."

I cracked up. "Yeah, right. 'Jamie, you hot *stallion*. I just gotta have some of your lovin'!'"

Caroline shrugged. "Hey, with a line like that, how could he resist?"

The three of us planned to hang out at the mall the next day so Caroline could take advantage of the no-limit credit card her dad got her after his last huge blowout with her mom.

In light of the information I'd shared, however, Caroline came up with a new plan. I'd go over to Jamie's house alone and tell him Caroline couldn't make it. Then, when he asked me what I wanted to do instead, it would be a ready-made segue into my answer: the nasty.

It all sounded good on paper, but when I got to Jamie's, I started to chicken out.

Partly it was his fault. When I told him Caroline wasn't coming, instead of asking what I wanted to do, he said, "Cool. How about helping me put together my new bookshelves?"

So instead of doing the humpity-pumpity, I was stuck wielding an Allen wrench, deciphering page after page of impossible Swedish instructions.

Jamie didn't seem to notice how funny I was acting. Or maybe he thought I was still upset about what happened with Noah on Friday. Either way, he hammered nails and adjusted shelves and did a five-minute improv bit on the inventor of the wrench in question—a guy named Allen who was born without thumbs—while I floundered around for an opening to bring up my plan.

By the time the shelves were finished and Jamie had stacked his gazillion comic books on them, I couldn't take it any longer.

Jamie stood up to brush the sawdust off his clothes. "Want to go to the mall now?" he asked.

No. I didn't.

I decided the best way to ask him was to just go ahead and put it out there. No fear, no pussyfooting around, no distractions. Just: do you want to sleep with me?

Only—

Maybe I should try flattery first.

"That is a volcanic ensemble you're wearing," I said, shamelessly borrowing Duckie's pickup line from *Pretty in Pink*.

Jamie cocked an eyebrow at me, glancing down at his decidedly dormant jeans and T-shirt. "Oh?"

"I just mean, you look—hot," I added, somewhat lamely.

"Hot?" Jamie echoed.

I gave him my sexiest smile. "White-hot."

Okay, I had to stop quoting that movie.

"I mean, sexy. Manly. Uh—*virile*."

Jamie looked at me, bewildered.

I shrugged. "What? Can't a girl enjoy a little eye candy?"

Jamie scrunched up his face. "No." He folded his arms across his chest. "Okay, so you're complimenting my clothes and my—uh—virility. You're referring to me as 'eye candy.' You clearly want something."

I gulped. "Uhhh . . ."

"You want . . . help cleaning out your closet," he guessed.

"Uh, no," I answered.

"You're going power shopping and you need me to . . . carry all your bags?" he tried again.

I shook my head, mute.

"Um . . . you want to borrow my DVD of *La dolce vita*?" Now he was really reaching.

Jamie blew out a breath, exasperated. "Fine. I give up. What *do* you want?"

Tell him. Tell him! my mind urged.

"I want . . ." I hesitated. "I want you to sleep with me!"

Jamie froze. He stared at me for a while, speechless. Then he threw back his head and roared with laughter.

I watched him from the bed, trying to figure out how to arrange my features so I'd look sexy.

Jamie laughed for about five minutes straight, then finally started to settle down.

"Yeah, right." He shook his head and wiped tears of merriment from his eyes. "You got me. I'll admit it. For a second I thought you were serious."

"I *am* serious," I said.

This set Jamie off again. I let out a frustrated breath, waiting for him to calm himself.

"I'm serious," I repeated. "I think we should have sex. Together. You and me. Now."

This time Jamie didn't laugh. *"Now?"*

"Well, fine. Maybe not this minute, but yeah. Why not?"

"Um, because it's crazy," he said.

"What's so crazy about it?"

Jamie shook his head, but I kept going, the words tumbling over each other in my haste to get them out. "Think about it, Jamie. It makes sense. We're both virgins. The last virgins left at school. We're friends. We like each other, so it wouldn't be weird. Our friendship would come first, and we could promise each other that nothing would change between us. Think about it. The way things are going now, neither of us has any better prospects, so—"

"Oh, that's romantic," he cut in.

"That's the point," I told him. "It's *not* romantic, which means all the pressure's off."

I paused. "Don't you want to know what it's like?"

"Of course," he said, "but come on. I thought you were all in love with Mr. One Man Pep Squad."

"Please. Noah and I don't stand a chance with the way things are now."

Jamie gave me a dubious look. "You really picture the two of us being a couple?"

"No. That's what I'm trying to tell you. We aren't going to start dating each other; we're just going to sleep with each other, then go back to being friends. Friends *who aren't virgins*."

Jamie stared at me. I could see that he was considering it. I held my breath, waiting to see what he'd say.

"Do you really think you could do that? Just go back to being friends?"

"Of course," I said.

"But what happens when we're about to do it and you freak out and run away? How'll we be friends after that?"

"That won't happen," I said, triumphant, "because if I *know* I'm about to do it *with you*, I won't go all crazy."

Jamie shook his head. "I don't know."

I let out a sigh. Nothing like having to beg a boy to have sex with you to kill the mood.

"Jamie. It's not a big deal. It's just sex. People do it every day. And it's time we caught up to the rest of the world."

Jamie was quiet for a second, absorbing this, then he smiled at me and shrugged. "What the hell? Let's do it."

I clapped and let out a squeal. "Really?"

Jamie frowned. "No. Not really. Try absolutely, positively *not*!"

9

e said what?" Caroline shrieked, digging her fingernails into my arm.

"He said he thought it sounded like a bad idea," I told her, "and excuse me, but—*ouch!*"

Caroline let go of my arm.

"I could kill Jamie," she seethed. "How could he say no? You know what, I'm going to go talk to him. I bet I can get him to change his mind."

She started into the school, but I grabbed the back of her shirt to stop her. "Don't. He's right. It was a stupid idea, and I'd rather forget the whole embarrassing thing."

After Jamie had turned me down, I beat a hasty retreat back to my house and finished the worst weekend of my life under the covers with a plate of brownies and the TV remote.

Pop!

I'd have been happy to pull a Hilly and never come out of my room again, but my parents said one hermit daughter was enough and made me come to school.

Jamie had called me last night to make sure I wasn't mad or embarrassed, so at least I wasn't afraid of seeing him.

It wasn't until I was changing back into my jeans and T-shirt after gym, however, that I remembered I had to see someone else.

Noah.

I had been so preoccupied with my Jamie plan that I didn't even think about what I was going to do in German class. The thought of facing Noah and, God forbid, discussing what had happened at the bonfire, was unbearable.

If I were a girl who cut classes, I would have spent the hour smoking or shoplifting or whatever those class-cutting types enjoy.

Sadly, that was not my thing. My only option, I decided, was to ignore Noah. I wouldn't sit by him, wouldn't look at him, and, with any luck, wouldn't have to deal with him at all.

At least, not until after I'd had a chance to think up some clever excuse for having taken matters—uh—*in hand*. When I arrived in class, I avoided Noah's gaze. I strode past him to the back of the room, where the science geeks sat.

I plonked my books on a desk near them and opened my notebook.

"What are *you* doing back here?" one of the geeks, a pimply chub in a Calvin and Hobbes T-shirt, asked.

Luckily, I had prepared for this question.

"Hi!" I said brightly. "I was wondering if you guys could help me."

They stared at me, expressionless, so I pushed on.

"I was reading up on Heisenberg, and I had some questions about his uncertainty principle."

I had ducked into the computer lab on my way to class and Googled *German scientists*.

I figured that maybe, if I could pretend to know about Otto Meyerhof and Fritz Strassmann and the rest of the science all-stars, the nerds would accept me as one of their own—and Noah would turn his attention somewhere else.

Calvin's ears pricked up at the mention of the famous scientist, and a little squirrelly kid who had been picking his nose next to us straightened up in his seat. He wiped the offending finger off on the side of his jeans. I quivered in disgust.

"What's your question?" Calvin asked in a voice that was almost friendly.

"Um." I tried to think up a question that wouldn't make me sound like an idiot. "What . . . *is* . . . the uncertainty principle?" I asked lamely.

"That you can't observe both the position and the momentum of an object at the same time," Professor Pick-a-nose told me.

Pop!

"Ah." I nodded wisely, but Calvin wasn't buying it.

"It's because the act of observing a system changes it?" he explained, in the same tone of voice I use to talk to my neighbor's two-year-old daughter, Mitzi.

"*Ohhhhh,*" I said, drawing the word out like the sun had just broken through the clouds. "*Now* I get it. Thanks."

He raised a dubious eyebrow. "Anything else?"

"Yeah. Wanna be conversation partners?" I asked, with a hopeful smile.

He regarded me for a minute. "Go away."

I sighed, then turned my attention to the goth girl seated on my other side.

"I hear Bauhaus might do a reunion tour," I offered.

She glowered at me, then got up and changed seats.

I glanced over at Noah—gorgeous, sexy, booger-free Noah—and made up my mind. Even though I had blown things with him romantically, maybe I could still salvage fifth period.

I took a deep breath and walked over to my old desk, holding up my hands in surrender.

"If I promise to keep my hands in sight at all times, can I sit with you?" I asked.

Noah smiled. "Just don't make any sudden movements."

I breathed a sigh of relief and slipped into my seat. "I'm sorry about what happened at the bonfire."

Noah shrugged. "It wasn't a big deal. At least, not until you made it one."

I grimaced. "I was embarrassed."

"Okay, but if you hadn't run away, we could have talked about it."

I gazed at him. Judging from his tone and expression, he seemed completely understanding.

"I know," I answered, dropping my eyes to my desktop. "I'm an idiot. And I'm just—I'm really, really shy about that stuff."

Noah paused for a second.

"You didn't *seem* shy," he said with a wicked grin. "Matter of fact, you seemed downright pushy. Or—*pully*, as the case may be."

"Shut up," I said, laughing but mortified. I gave him a playful slap on his arm.

"Ah!" Noah shrieked, pretending to cower. "You promised you wouldn't touch me!"

"Stop!" I said, laughing harder.

Herr Robinson frowned at me from the front of the room, where he was conjugating the verb *sein* on the blackboard.

"Entschuldigung! Möchten Sie Deutsch lernen?" he asked.

No idea.

"Ja?" I answered. Apparently satisfied, Herr Robinson turned back to the board.

Noah leaned toward me. "Seriously, though. Let's start over, okay? Because even though the bonfire was a bust, I'm new here, and I need all the friends I can get."

My heart sank a little.

The dreaded *f* word. Noah wanted to be *friends*. I couldn't say I was surprised, after the way I'd acted.

I wanted to plunge a number-two pencil into my heart, but instead I gave Noah a big smile. "I suppose that means you need a conversation partner too?"

"You bet." He smiled at me, then flipped open his textbook. "Maybe you can come over after school and we can get a jump on the translations."

"Um, sure," I answered.

Then Herr Robinson started the lesson.

Okay, so maybe Noah only wants to be friends, I thought. *That's fine for now. Because once I get this whole scared-of-sex thing taken care of, anything can happen.*

I glanced over at Noah.

Anything.

"I don't get why you'd *want* to stay friends with him," Jamie said later that afternoon. "He's such a—a hall monitor."

We were standing by our lockers after last class, and I had just told Jamie and Caroline that no, I wouldn't be accompanying them to Pizza Hut, because I had other plans.

"He's the first ex-boyfriend I've ever had that I'm not too embarrassed to talk to!" I repeated. "It's like . . . a miracle."

"First of all, you guys had, like, half of a date, so I don't know if *ex-boyfriend* applies," Jamie said.

I opened my mouth to protest.

"But even if it does," he hurried to add, "why would you want to hang out with a guy like *that*?"

My answer was drowned out by a burst of cheering.

"*P-S-Y! C-H-E-D!* Psyched is what we wanna be!"

Rick Fielding, Jamie's arch-nemesis, came strolling down the hall with a couple of his thuggish goon friends.

They were on their way to practice, and the cheerleaders were accompanying them, clapping and chanting.

"Get psyched! Aw' right! Aw' right, get psyched!"

As they passed us by, Rick nudged Jamie with his shoulder, just hard enough to knock him off balance and make him drop his calculus book.

Jamie stooped to pick it up, but before he could reach it, one of the goons kicked it, sending Jamie's homework sprawling down the hall.

"Stupid juicers," Jamie muttered.

The rest of the jocks strode past, not even glancing in Jamie's direction. I rescued his textbook, and Caroline managed to capture the homework before too many people had trampled on it.

"God, what losers," Caroline said, staring daggers at their receding backs.

"Eh, the steroids'll get 'em," I said. "You know, I've heard it shrinks your you-know-what to—" I held my thumb and forefinger up about an inch apart.

It was a joke, but Jamie didn't laugh.

"I *hate* those guys," he said, "and now you're becoming friends with one of them."

"Who, Noah?" I asked, surprised. "He's nothing like Rick."

"He's on the lacrosse team," Jamie argued.

"Big deal. Juliet Hammond plays flute in orchestra, and we're nothing like her," I said.

"That is completely different," Jamie insisted.

"No, it's not." I held firm.

"Come on, Marit, you can't actually *like* him," Jamie argued. "He's a *joiner*."

He said this the same way you might say *child molester* or *crackhead*.

"You've spent the last *eleven years* making fun of people like him," Jamie said.

This was true. However—

"Why are you being such a jerk?" I asked, more curious than mad.

"He's just bitter," Caroline piped up. "Because he had a chance to lose his virginity and blew it."

"Caroline!" Jamie and I both turned on her.

I gritted my teeth. "You promised me you wouldn't mention it."

"I can't believe you told *Caroline*," Jamie yelped, affronted.

"Why wouldn't she tell me?" Caroline asked. She narrowed her eyes at Jamie. "You know, maybe it's a good thing you guys aren't hooking up. You could end up keeping secrets from me."

"There's nothing to keep secret," Jamie snapped, "because we're not doing anything."

"Then stop acting like a jerk," Caroline countered.

"*You're* the jerk!" Jamie told her.

"Oh my God!" I covered my ears with my hands. "This is completely ridiculous. Jamie, I'm sorry I told Caroline, but it's not like anything happened anyway. Caroline, I asked *you* not to mention it, but now that's done, so can we all just move on and pretend I never asked Jamie to have sex?"

They both looked at me for a second, then Jamie turned back to Caroline. "And I *so* don't care about being a virgin."

"Yeah. Keep telling yourself that."

I threw my hands in the air, exasperated. "You guys work this out for yourselves. I've got to go meet my brand-new friend Noah."

I slammed my locker door shut and strode off toward the student parking lot, leaving my dearest and their insanity behind.

10

D o you think it's too late to switch to Spanish?"
I asked, pushing my textbook away from me and leaning back in my chair to stretch.

Noah shook his head. "Not possible. If you did, we'd never find out if Ilsa and Klaus made it to the train station on time."

"You're right," I agreed. "I wouldn't be able to sleep, not knowing."

We'd been sitting at Noah's kitchen table, doing our homework, for the last three hours.

I was, to coin a phrase, German-ed out.

"You want to take a break?" Noah asked, getting up and carrying our empty soda cans to the garbage.

"Sure." I closed my book and followed him into the living room.

"I just got GTA: San Andreas for my PS2," he called over his shoulder.

Your wha for your who?

I frowned. "I'm, uh, not really sure what you just said."

Noah grinned. "Grand Theft Auto: San Andreas? It's a video game?"

I shrugged.

I spent most of my free time painting with my dad or watching obscure art films with Jamie and Caroline.

Video games? Not really a part of the program.

"It's the one where you get to steal cars and shoot cops," Noah said. "Want to play?"

"Um—" I hesitated.

"It's not hard," he said, grinning. "I can show you."

I stalled again, then decided that I might as well be honest. "Really? This is so stupid, but—I'm sort of against the whole gun thing, even if it is just a game."

Noah studied me for a second. "Well, you don't have to *shoot* anyone. You can also run them over with a car or beat them with a tire iron."

I stared at him, incredulous.

"Joking!" he told me.

I exhaled. Thank God.

"The first time I played, I felt kind of bad about it too," Noah said.

"Really?" I asked.

"Yeah. I like to think of myself as a force for good."

I tried not to grin. "A force for good . . . like a superhero?"

"Yeah. Me and Tobey Maguire." Noah looked off into the distance. "He was so heroic in *Seabiscuit*."

I cracked up, and Noah handed me the controller. "C'mon. It's really just a game. And it's fun."

For a second I wondered what Caroline and Jamie would think.

Then I thought, *Screw it.*

"Hit the play button," I told Noah. "I'm taking you down."

The game actually *was* pretty fun, even though I kept accidentally killing my character, Carl.

But even better? I was hanging out with Noah and *not* acting like a mental patient.

Really, it was amazing how relaxed I could be when I knew sex was off the table.

I still felt kind of giggly when he smiled or when our arms bumped against each other. I was only human, after all. But since Noah had flat-out stated he just wanted me to be a *friend*, I shoved all those giggly feelings to the back of my mind and was able to just act like myself.

This is why I need to lose my virginity, I decided, glancing at

Noah and inadvertently killing Carl again. *So I can be this calm and in control—with a boy I actually have a shot with.*

An hour later I had busted out of jail, held up a burger joint, and propositioned a hooker. To be honest, I felt pretty good about it. I was in the middle of trying to steal a cop car when Noah's front door opened.

A little kid who was dressed up like a robot came zooming in. He raced over to the couch and hurled himself on top of Noah, knocking the controller out of my hand and sending Carl to his grave for the final time.

Noah laughed and hugged the kid, then swooped him through the air and set him down on the floor in front of us.

"Who are you?" the kid asked, fixing his gaze on me.

"I'm Marit," I told him. "Are you a Power Ranger?"

"No. I'm a Bionicle! Duh!" he shouted, and raced out of the room.

"That's my brother, Charlie," Noah said.

"Cute. But why is he in a costume?" I asked.

Noah shrugged, amused. "He refuses to take it off, and I guess my stepmom just got tired of arguing with him."

A second later a pretty blond woman poked her head into the room.

"Hey, Karen," Noah called. "This is my friend Marit. We were just doing our homework together."

Karen's gaze ticked over to the TV. "So I see," she said with a wry smile. "Dinner will ready in about half an hour—Marit, will you be staying?"

Noah gave me a "why not?" look, so I smiled. "Thanks."

I called home and checked with my mom. Thirty minutes later I was back at Noah's kitchen table, with a plate of chicken and mashed potatoes, listening to Charlie wax on at length about what he wanted to be for Halloween.

"I'm gonna be King Kong," he said. "Or maybe Darth Maul, except only if I can have a real double light saber, not two regular light sabers taped together."

I decided to take another shot at winning him over. "You don't want to dress up as a Bionicle?" I asked.

Charlie sighed, as if it caused him physical pain to talk to someone as dim-witted as me.

"I *am* a Bionicle," he explained. "I don't need to dress up as one."

The rest of his family chuckled as I mentally crossed *nanny* off my list of future career possibilities.

"You've still got plenty of time to decide," Noah's father told Charlie. "Halloween's more than a month away."

"Yeah, but when it's here, can we go to the haunted house again like last year?"

"Well, we'll have to find a different one," Karen said, "but I'm sure it'll be just as scary."

"There was an actual haunted house in the neighborhood where we used to live in Texas," Noah explained. "It was this gigantic mansion owned by this rich old lady—"

"She was over a hundred years old!" Charlie interjected, his eyes widening at the memory.

"It was haunted by the spirits of soldiers who had died at the Alamo, and every year on Halloween the lady would let people tour the house and see if they could spot the ghosts."

"I saw a ghost!" Charlie said.

"You did not," Noah answered.

"I did. I saw a ghost and I punched it and got ghost brains all over my hand."

Noah rumpled his little brother's hair.

"We have an entire haunted street," I told Charlie. "It's called Irwin Road, and it's out in the middle of nowhere, in the woods. Every time someone drives down it, it changes shape, and the only people who live on it are devil worshipers!"

Charlie's eyes got even wider, and he grabbed Noah's arm. "Whoa! Can we go there? Can we go to Irwin Road with Marit tonight?"

Ha! I thought. *Got 'im! Third time's a charm.*

Karen shook her head. "Tonight you're taking a bath, then bedtime."

Charlie's chin started to quiver, so Noah gave him a little chuck on his shoulder. "Tell you what, maybe Marit can show me where Irwin Road is tonight, and then I'll take you there this weekend."

"Yay!" Charlie turned back to his mashed potatoes, and Noah smiled across the table.

"That cool?" he asked me.

"Sure. Only—I'm not exactly sure how to get there—Jamie always drives."

"So? Let's call him and see if he wants to go."

"Really?" I gulped.

"Why not?" Noah said.

Because Jamie thinks you're a hall monitor, I thought.

Then it occurred to me—Noah was, for certain, a cool guy. If I'd ever had any doubts about it, spending the evening with him had proved them wrong.

He was sweet, funny, and smart—even if he didn't like the exact same things my friends and I did. If Jamie and Caroline actually spent time with Noah, they'd see for themselves how excellent he was.

And what better place for them to get to know each other than far away from school, where, with a bit of luck, the opportunities for snarkiness would be at a minimum?

"Yeah. Why not?" I agreed. "What's the worst that could happen?"

I called Caroline first since *she* didn't seem to have any problems with Noah and, in our group, majority rules.

She said going for a drive down Irwin Road sounded genius, especially since Jamie had been forcing her to watch *Russian Ark*, and as far as she was concerned, even a pillow polo tournament would be a better way to spend the evening.

They arrived at Noah's house a few minutes later, and while Jamie didn't look thrilled, he did shake the hand Noah offered without making any comments about the ludicrousness of teenagers shaking hands.

He did, however, raise an eyebrow at me—just to let me know he was thinking it.

"How'd you get him to come?" I whispered to Caroline as we were walking out to the car.

"I promised him we'd all watch *Russian Ark* tomorrow—"

I shrugged. "That's not so bad—"

"*With* the director's commentary *and* the DVD extras."

I groaned. Bor-ring. But it would be worth it if, at the end of this little field trip, everyone liked each other.

Noah and I piled into the backseat of Jamie's old Honda and he pulled out into the street.

"Ready to see Greenwich's only urban legend?" Caroline asked.

Noah nodded. "I had no idea Connecticut was such a hot spot for devil worshipers."

"Well, they mostly come for the tax breaks," Jamie said.

Caroline turned halfway around in the passenger seat so

she could talk to us. "No, seriously, it's really scary. The road's really curvy, so you never know what's around the next bend. Lots of people have crashed their cars because the road turns unexpectedly—"

"And then the devil worshipers come and use the people trapped in their cars as human sacrifices!" I added.

"Man. That would make a great horror movie," Noah observed.

For the first time since we got in the car, Jamie perked up. "Only if the devil worshipers are children. *Nothing* is scarier than an evil child."

"No way." Noah shook his head. "*Mirrors*. That's the scariest thing in a horror movie."

"Oh my God, like that one where the person looks in the mirror and they only see the back of their head!" Caroline said. "What was that movie?"

"There have been, like, half a dozen where that happened," I told her.

"I just meant the way you always see someone in the mirror behind you," Noah said.

"Oh, man. What if you saw an *evil child* in the mirror behind you?" Jamie asked. "Super-terrifying."

We all agreed. I smiled. This was going well.

"I tell you, ever since I saw *The Ring*, I can barely even be in a room with a TV," I offered.

Noah turned to me. "Have you seen the original, in Japanese? *Ringu*? It's way more scary."

"Which is why I will never see it," I told him.

"Oh, but the director, Hideo Nakata, is brilliant," Noah said.

"You like Nakata?!" Jamie asked, craning around in his seat to look at Noah.

"Careful!" Caroline said.

Jamie swerved, narrowly missing a street sign. He re-adjusted the rearview mirror so he could see Noah clearly.

"Yeah, I love him," Noah said. "But Nakagawa's way better. Have you seen *Kaiidan*?"

"Only a crap VHS copy," Jamie answered.

"I have it on DVD—I'll lend it to you," Noah said.

I leaned back in my seat, a fizzy, happy feeling in my head. I had no idea who or what *Kaiidan* was, but I couldn't have planned the conversation any better.

Jamie and Noah compared obscure horror films the whole drive until we got to the turnoff to Irwin Road.

I didn't believe the stories, of course, but I still felt a little shiver up my spine. Irwin Road was a spooky place. It cut through a dense section of woods, with a wall of trees pressed up against both sides of the road.

The branches formed a dark, tangled canopy overhead, blocking out any trace of moonlight. The road was a series of hairpin turns, without a single straight stretch longer than fifty feet.

What made it *especially* scary was that someone had nailed odd hexes and crosses and symbols to the trunks of the trees, at just the right level so your headlights would glint off them as you rounded the curves.

The first time we'd ever driven down it, right after Jamie got his license, someone had hung a noose from one of the overhead branches. It slapped our windshield as we drove under it. I screamed so hard it was a miracle I didn't wet my pants.

At that moment I wondered—why had I agreed to come here again?

Noah put a hand on my knee and squeezed. "Here we go," he whispered.

Oh yeah. That was why.

Jamie shut off the radio as he turned his car onto Irwin Road. We all rolled down our windows, as is the custom.

It was beyond dark, the trees absorbing the feeble light from our headlights. As we rolled through, we heard odd rustlings and strange snapping noises in the woods. It was a scene straight out of *The Blair Witch Project*, only *I* wasn't dumb enough to get out of the car.

The cold air whipped through the open windows, and I started shivering.

We went around the first three bends in silence, but as

Jamie started to turn the car into the fourth, trees sprang up blocking our path, and the road swooped in an unexpected direction.

We all gasped as Jamie yanked hard on the steering wheel, getting the car back on the road. As it straightened out, the headlights hit a shiny squiggle nailed onto one of the trees. The odd symbol flashed as the headlights struck it, the reflection momentarily blinding us.

I shrieked, and Jamie shushed me. "The devil vorshipers vill hear you!" he said in a Dracula voice.

We all giggled.

As we neared the place where Irwin Road reconnected with the highway, Caroline let out a sigh. "I think we made it."

Noah nudged me with his elbow, then leaned his head close to mine.

"Watch this," he whispered in my ear.

He snuck his hand out of his open window and stretched his arm forward to the passenger side where Caroline was sitting. Even in the dark, I could see his grin.

He reached inside Caroline's window—and grabbed her shoulder!

"Eee!" Caroline screamed. She jumped about a mile into the air and swatted hysterically at the place where Noah had touched her. "Oh my God, what was that? What was that?"

Noah and I howled with laughter. Jamie, knowing

immediately what had happened, laughed himself and nearly ran off the road for real.

Finally Caroline stopped screaming long enough to notice that we were all cracking up. She whirled around in her seat to face us.

"Was that *you*?" she shouted, looking like she was torn between laughing or murdering us.

"I'm sorry," Noah gasped, holding up his hands in surrender. "I just couldn't resist."

We were still laughing when we finally made it back to the safety of the highway. Jamie pulled into a Dunkin' Donuts so we could soothe our shaky nerves with powdered sugar.

Caroline and I grabbed a booth as the boys went up to the counter to get our snacks. I was dying to ask her what she thought of Noah, but I didn't want to risk being overheard, so I just raised my eyebrows in question.

She answered with a smile.

Jamie came over to the table and slid into the seat next to Caroline. Noah took a seat next to me.

"Hey, I was thinking," Noah said as he set the tray of doughnuts down on the table, "we should start a film club at Sterling."

Uh-oh. Things had been going so well. I'd thought we were home free. I caught Jamie and Caroline exchanging a quick glance and said a silent prayer that everything wouldn't fall to pieces now.

Noah settled in next to me and draped his arm casually across the back of the seat behind my shoulders. "I bet we could get Mr. Decker to sponsor it, since he already runs the drama club anyway. What do you think?"

Jamie's eyes flicked from Noah's face to the arm he had slung behind my shoulders.

"I don't know," he said carefully. "Seems to me Mr. Decker's already got a lot on his plate. Isn't he directing a play or something?"

Noah nodded. "*Guys and Dolls.* I'm trying out for the lead—Sky Masterson. A bunch of the guys I met from the team are auditioning, and so are their girlfriends. Are any of you going for a role?"

Caroline snorted, then winced as I kicked her under the table. "Jamie and Marit are the two most tone-deaf people on the East Coast," she said to Noah, covering. "And while *I* happen to have a lovely singing voice"—here it was my turn to snort—"I'm afraid I'm completely booked every day after school."

"With what?" Noah asked.

Caroline made a vague gesture. "Many pressing engagements. Life and all that."

Noah shot me a look—*Is she kidding?* I gave him a weak smile in return.

"Caroline's right," Jamie interjected. "We have our own

interests. We leave after-school activities to the people who like following the crowd."

The table descended into a heavy silence.

Okay. This little social experiment was over.

I stretched my arms over my head in a gigantic yawn. "Gosh, it's getting late. You guys ready to go?"

All three of them looked at me and shrugged, then got up from the table and headed toward the door.

Jamie dropped Noah off first. Noah said good night to all of us, then pointed his fingers like double guns at Jamie. "Let me know what you decide about the film club, okay, dude?"

"Will do"—Jamie smiled weakly, giving Noah a lame "double guns" back—"dude."

Noah waved, and Jamie pulled out of his driveway onto the street.

We rode in silence for a few seconds, then Caroline turned around to face me.

"You're right," she said. "He's nice."

"*Thank* you," I said pointedly.

"Didn't you think he was nice, Jamie?" she prompted.

"Oh, absolutely," Jamie answered. "And I'll be sure to tell him that at our inaugural *film club meeting*."

"Stop," I said.

"What?" Jamie asked, all innocent-like.

"Don't make fun of him."

"Hey, we could not have been better behaved," Caroline said. "Even when he was lobbing them right at us—"

"Like when?"

She stared at me meaningfully. *"Sky Masterson?"*

Okay, that *was* pretty bad. Noah was, like, chronically involved. But still—

"But he's not a *bad guy*, right? To have as a friend?"

"Of course not," Caroline said.

"As long as you don't mind lemmings," Jamie muttered. He turned the radio up, and we were quiet the rest of the way home.

11

Jamie dropped Caroline and me off at the foot of our driveways, where my front lawn and hers butt up against each other. He drove off as Caroline and I were still saying good night.

But as I was walking into my bedroom, I heard the squeak of the back gate and looked out to see Jamie waving up at my window.

Five minutes later he was leaning against the kitchen counter, watching as I stirred milk and chocolate on the stove, making cocoa. He hadn't mentioned why he had come back, so we just stood there, listening to the clock radio above the refrigerator.

Some eighties song was playing. Journey, I thought. Or maybe just that lead guy, without the rest of the band.

Jamie took a deep breath.

I looked over at him, and he smiled oddly.

"Marit, listen—" he started, then paused.

"Ye-e-e-es?" I said, drawing the word out into about six syllables.

This usually cracks Jamie up. But he didn't smile.

"Do you really like that guy?" he said, completely out of nowhere.

"Noah?" I asked.

He nodded.

"I'd worship *anybody* who made German a little less torturous," I answered.

Jamie shifted foot to foot, clearly uncomfortable. "Don't make me say this; it's so *Degrassi*," he pleaded.

"Say what?"

He gave an impatient little wriggle. "Do you . . . *like him*, like him?"

I shrugged. I was disappointed, but the truth was the truth. "We're just friends."

"Even though you had a huge crush on him," Jamie pressed, "and now you're hanging out and all?"

I wasn't sure where Jamie was going with all of this, but . . . "That ship has sailed," I told him. "I blew my chances with him at the bonfire. We're just friends now. Nothing more."

"Good." Jamie stared down at the counter, the tips of his ears turning pink.

"I was thinking about what you asked me," he said.

"About . . . ?"

"About—about us being each other's first time."

I turned away from the stove and stared at him, hard. "Don't tease me," I said. "I'm still completely embarrassed about—"

"No—" Jamie reached out a hand, rested it on my forearm. His fingers were warm against my skin. "I'm not teasing you—I was just thinking. I was thinking . . . yes."

"Yes?" I whispered. My mind was moving too slowly—I couldn't catch up with my own thoughts.

"Yes," Jamie repeated. "I mean, if you still want to."

All at once I couldn't breathe. I forced myself to think logically. The main reason Noah and I were "just friends" was because of the big V. Even if it was too late for me and Noah, I still needed to do it. Otherwise I was bound to send the *next* perfect guy packing.

"Of course I still want to," I told Jamie. "Only, are you positive?"

Jamie gave me a crooked little smile. "Here—"

He turned so he was facing me, moving in as close as he could, so close I could feel a prickling sensation up and down my body, static electricity crackling between us. He looked me right in the eyes, and I laughed nervously.

"Jamie—"

"Wait," he said softly. "Let me just . . ."

He leaned forward until his lips were less than an inch from mine. Both of our eyes were still open, so I shut mine, and when I peeked a second later, he'd shut his too.

He leaned forward and grazed my lips with his. It was the sort of chaste kiss you'd get from your brother, so I tilted my head a tiny bit to the right and, feeling like I was about to jump off a cliff, pressed my mouth against his, opening my lips slightly.

His mouth was warm and soft, and his hands tightened on my waist. Jamie pulled me closer into him, our bodies resting against each other's. I could feel his heart beating through his shirt.

For a second I flinched, thinking about how he could probably feel my boobs squashed against his chest.

But then I felt something press against my leg.

Well, if Jamie wasn't self-conscious, I didn't need to be either.

Jamie kissed me harder. My head was swimming.

I can't believe we're doing this! I thought.

After a few minutes Jamie pulled away.

"Wow," he said softly. "That was—"

"—nice?" I finished, having a hard time catching my breath.

"Mind-blowing."

He darted his eyes sideways toward the stairs leading up to my room, then lifted a shoulder in a questioning shrug. "So, should we . . . ?"

"My parents are home!" I said.

"We could lock the door."

I shook my head. "I want to have sex, not put my life on the line." I thought about it for a minute, then had a flash of inspiration. "This weekend my parents are taking Hilly up to Boston to look at schools. Caroline was going to stay over to keep me company, but . . ."

"I'm good company," Jamie said.

"Okay." I nodded. "Then that's when we'll . . . do it."

Jamie and I grinned at each other, then he lightly kissed me one more time. "Bye," he murmured, and walked out the door.

I stayed where I was, a million thoughts swirling around in my brain. A million feelings fluttering through me.

Only the smell of the cocoa, burning on the stove, jolted me out of my trance.

I switched off the burner, put the pot in the sink, then went upstairs and got into bed, even though I knew I would never, ever be able to get to sleep tonight.

"What is going on with you guys?" Caroline asked. She

looked from Jamie to me, then shoved about six french fries into her mouth at once.

Jamie and I both shrugged, completely innocent. "Nothing," I answered, pulling the plate a little closer so she couldn't eat them all.

"Then how come you've been acting like pod people all day?" she mumbled as she chewed.

The three of us were spread out across one of the molded plastic tables of the Westport Mall food court. The glorious dieting potential of second-period lunch had devolved into the tragic reality of after-school starvation, and we were already on our second round of snacks.

All day long I had looked for the right time to tell Caroline about Jamie's and my decision. But every time I started to tell her, Nina or Abby or someone would interrupt, and honestly, I didn't want anyone else to know.

Now that we finally had some privacy, it seemed wrong to just blurt it out with no preamble.

"We're acting completely normal," I insisted, reaching across the table for the plate of nachos. "You're the one who—"

"We kissed!" Jamie burst out all of a sudden. "We kissed and we're going to have sex!"

Okay. So maybe not so difficult after all.

Caroline's mouth fell open. She grabbed our arms, and her face lit up. "Oh my God! That's fantastic! I can't believe it!"

"Neither can I," Jamie admitted.

Caroline clapped. "This is so perfect! You guys are going to make the best couple! Only"—she stopped suddenly, her whole demeanor drooping—"when you two start dating, I'm going to be totally left out."

"Oh, we're not going to *date*," I reassured her, trying to inconspicuously nab the chip situated directly under the guacamole, "we're just . . . sleeping together."

"Really?" Caroline asked doubtfully.

"That's the plan," Jamie said. He attacked my nacho with one of his own, stealing back a giant glob. "Don't worry, Caroline. Nothing's going to change."

"We made a pact," I reassured her. "We're going to stay friends—exactly how we are now."

Caroline thought about this for a minute. "And you won't start having all sorts of annoying secrets and private jokes?"

"No way," Jamie said.

"We'll tell you every single excruciating detail about it," I added.

"Well, I don't need to hear *every* detail." Caroline grinned, snatching up the very last nacho. "Just the dirty ones!"

The rest of the week passed in a blur. By the time my parents and Hilly left for Boston on Friday afternoon, I was a wreck!

It was just Jamie, but still—this was a monumental thing I was doing. I wanted everything to be perfect, since I would remember this night for the rest of my life.

I spent an hour in the shower, borrowed my mom's Aveda body scrub, and shampooed my hair twice. I tried shaving my legs super-thoroughly and ended up getting about a million little cuts on them, which made me rethink the bikini line.

I painted my fingernails a soft pink and my toenails a more electric shade. I put in the magnetic rhinestone belly-button ring that Caroline gave me for my last birthday and slipped on the prettiest underwear that I own, a lavender lace set from Victoria's Secret that I had to beg my mom to let me buy. I actually wanted it in black, but she said that was too *advanced* for a girl my age, which I took to mean she's in total denial about the real world.

Then I went into my closet to decide what to wear.

My closet is the best thing about my room. It's a gigantic walk-in, with a mural I painted over the walls and ceiling. There are pictures of birds and flowers, abstract shapes, and anything else that comes into my head. It's my masterpiece.

I keep my clothes on a rolling metal garment rack, like you see in old movies about New York City, but the truth is, a lot of my clothes end up scattered all over the floor or lying in heaps on top of every available surface.

Luckily, I knew exactly where to find my turquoise dress

with the spaghetti straps, the one I'd rechristened my "doin' it with Jamie" dress.

I put on enough lip gloss, blush, and mascara to make me look a little less ghostly, tried to tame my Pam Grier mega-curls with a handful of gel, and gave myself a generous spritz of Tommy Girl.

Then I headed down the hall and slipped into Hilly's room.

I took a deep breath and pulled open the bottom drawer of Hilly's dresser. Underneath her bathing suits and too-small summer dresses, I knew she kept a box of condoms.

Turns out, it was a really big box. It was supposed to hold thirty-six condoms. Thirty-six!

I grabbed a condom from the box and swiped a second just in case.

I was about to turn and leave when something else caught my eye. An old cassette tape with a fresh Post-it note stuck to it.

Marit—play this, it said in Hilly's angular handwriting. *Thad's mix. Guaranteed to set the mood.*

A little winking smiley face ended the note.

A picture of Hilly's boyfriend, Thad, popped into my head, but I quickly shook it off. The thought of him getting busy with my sister was too gross to contemplate.

So I grabbed the tape and got the hell out of Hilly's room before I ruined sex for myself for all eternity.

Jamie arrived at my front door at eight o'clock on the button. He stood in the foyer, his jacket in his hand, looking so self-conscious and formal that I considered calling the whole thing off.

"Hi," I finally said.

"Hi."

I couldn't think up anything to say next. We both squirmed in silent discomfort, neither of us able to figure out how to get things started. Finally Jamie reached into his backpack and pulled out a bottle of peach schnapps.

"I thought we might need something to help us loosen up," he said.

"Hallelujah," I cheered. "I'll get the orange juice."

Jamie, Caroline, and I don't usually drink. Hilly sneaks us

the occasional beer, and every time we have dinner at Jamie's house, his parents make a big deal out of serving us each a glass of wine. But I'm not crazy about it. I don't like feeling that loss of control.

Comes in handy, though, when you're about to get it on with your best friend.

We carried our drinks into my bedroom, and I sat down on my bed. It was just like every other time we've hung out in my room except for some reason, we couldn't find anything to say to each other.

We polished off our drinks, and my head felt pleasantly cloudy. I stuck Hilly's cassette in my ancient tape player and pressed play.

An old soul tune, "Let's Stay Together," by Al Green, came out of the speakers.

I took a deep breath. *Okay, this is chill.*

I turned around and—*oh my God, Jamie was taking his clothes off!*

He pulled his Franz Ferdinand T-shirt over his head and started to undo the button on his jeans.

He glanced over at me and stopped.

"Um, are you just going to stare at me like that?" he asked, his voice higher than usual.

"I wasn't *staring*," I said, my voice also wobbly. "God. Pardon me for having *eyes*."

"Well, are you going to get undressed too?" he asked.

I squirmed. "Uh . . . maybe we can, like, ease into it?"

Jamie thought about this, then sat down on the edge of my bed. "Okay, how about we play strip poker?"

"I don't know . . ." I said, making a face.

Poker was number one on my list of Things I Can't Understand People Liking, along with *American Idol*, Ugg boots, and those Japanese mochi ice cream balls.

Also, I wasn't sure I wanted my First Time to start off with a card game.

Jamie rolled his eyes, knowing exactly what I was thinking. "Let's play something else, then. I never? Truth or dare?"

"Truth or dare," I said. "I'll start. Dare."

"I dare you to kiss me," Jamie said.

I leaned over and lightly pressed my lips against his. Jamie lifted a hand to my cheek. He caressed my face with his thumb.

I was tense; I'll admit it. A little voice in my head kept screaming, *What are you doing? This is Jamie!*

I shut my eyes tight, but I couldn't figure out a way to muzzle it.

After a moment I decided to focus not on the situation—me, Jamie, my bedroom—but on the kiss itself. The feeling of lips and tongue. Jamie's slight stubble rubbing against my skin.

That sweet fizzy feeling filled my brain. I could feel myself melting, relaxing.

All right. Now we were getting somewhere.

Jamie broke away and looked at me through slitted eyes. "Dare."

"I dare you to—" Did I have the guts to say it? "Take off your jeans."

Jamie stood up and pulled off his jeans, looking somewhere just to the left of me as he did it. Underneath, he was wearing pale blue boxers. They were obviously brand-new—they still had the creases from the packaging pressed into them.

Okay. I had seen him in bathing suits that covered less. Nothing to freak out about . . . yet.

He tossed the jeans onto my desk chair, then gave me a shy smile. "Your turn."

I gulped. "Dare."

"I dare you to—take off your dress."

I squeezed my eyes closed, steeling my nerves. I pulled my dress over my head and caught a glimpse of myself in the dresser mirror. Oh my God. My mom was right. My underwear did look . . . *advanced*.

Maybe I should've stuck with a sports bra. I panicked. Then I saw the look on Jamie's face.

Hmmm. Maybe not.

Jamie hooked his thumbs in the waistband of his boxers, then stopped. "Do we—should we, uh, get in bed?"

"You didn't dare me," I said, the words sticking in my throat.

"I'm through playing," he answered softly.

I pulled back the covers on the bed. "Can we . . . turn the lights out?"

Jamie reached over and hit the switch.

Darkness settled over the room.

We got into bed, and then all at once it was happening.

Jamie pulled me close and kissed my neck. I focused only on the sensation—it was easier to do in the dark. And it felt good.

He ran his hands down my arms, over my back. I rested my hands on his chest, moved them to his shoulders.

"Marit," Jamie whispered.

I shivered, but for once it wasn't out of fear. I knew exactly where this was going, and I wasn't terrified. I was okay, and I wasn't going anywhere.

Jamie kissed me a bit longer, then reached around for my bra. He struggled with the hook so long I was worried that the weekend would be over before he'd manage to get it undone.

So I shifted my weight onto one side and reached my hand back behind me. "Here," I whispered, and unsnapped it with a single flick.

Pop!

Jamie slipped my bra off. I closed my eyes and felt his warm hands on me, around me. My whole body seemed to vibrate from his touch.

I slipped off the rest, and then I was totally naked. Naked in bed with a boy.

Unbelievable.

I heard a rip of paper, and Jamie fiddled with a condom, slipping it on.

He positioned himself on top of me, then stopped.

"Are you okay?" he murmured, and I nodded, even though he couldn't see me in the dark. I wrapped my arms around him and, amazed at my daring, ran my hand all the way down his back and over his butt.

Jamie let out a groan, then reached down.

My God, I thought, *this is it!* I was officially doing it! I held my breath, waiting.

But it wasn't going in.

Instead Jamie kept bumping against my thigh. I could feel his muscles tensing as he groped around, getting frustrated. Was I supposed to be doing something to help? Was I doing it wrong? He pushed hard against my leg, then let out an angry breath. "Damn it."

"Jamie?" I asked, not really sure what my question was.

"It's not working!"

"Here," I said; then I reached down.

Jamie sucked in his breath.

I have to admit, it felt different than I would've imagined. I always thought that when boys "got hard," they meant really hard, like a rock, but it felt more like I was holding a tube of cookie dough.

I held him really gingerly, with two fingers, and moved him over to where he needed to go.

Jamie started pushing against me and—

"Ow!"

He stopped moving. "Sorry."

"No, it's okay," I whispered. He started pushing again.

"It's not—" he mumbled.

I tried to help. "Wait—here—I'll—"

Jamie pushed farther.

"Ow! Hold on, I—"

"Oh God."

"What is it?"

"God! Oh God! God!"

Suddenly Jamie stiffened. He collapsed on my chest, breathing hard.

I held my breath, waiting for the moment I would be swept away, carried off, delirious with passion and desire. At the very least, I expected the warm wave of intensity I felt when I was by myself.

But none of that happened.

Pop!

Instead Jamie's arm rested on my hair so I couldn't move my head. My head buzzed, like I had stood up too fast. I tasted salt on my lips and heard the blood rushing in my ears.

I realized I was still holding my breath—and as I let it out, Jamie shuddered. He rolled off me.

And just like that—I wasn't a virgin anymore.

I don't know," I said, shrugging. "It was okay, I guess."

"Marit!" Caroline shrieked so loudly that the middle-aged ladies sitting at the table next to ours gave us the evil eye. "You can't just tell me it was *okay*. I want details!"

I frowned and fiddled with the napkin on my lap. "Really, there's not much to tell."

"Oh, I don't believe that," Caroline teased. "You *were* walking kind of funny, you know."

"Ha, ha," I deadpanned.

It was the next morning, and Caroline was so eager to hear about my night that she'd called me practically before the sun was up. She'd insisted we meet for breakfast at Denny's, which was the only restaurant open on Saturday at such an ungodly hour.

I thought I'd be eager to tell her about it, but when it came time to actually dish the dirt, I found myself tongue-tied. It wasn't that I was shy or embarrassed, but I guess I didn't know how I felt about it myself.

Everyone had made such a big deal about the whole thing—including me. But in the end, I wasn't sure it was all that momentous. It was more like, *that* was what I so desperately needed to get out of the way?

I didn't understand.

It felt like there was something missing.

Caroline raised her hot chocolate and took a swig. "So, tell me! Did you like it?"

"I'm not sure," I said. "I mean, I'm happy I got it over with, but . . ."

"But?" Caroline prodded.

"But it kind of hurt."

"It always does," Caroline said.

I felt my eyes go wide. *"Always?"* I asked, horrified.

"No. I meant the first time always hurts," she clarified. "It gets better the more you do it."

Well, that was a relief. Because even when it wasn't hurting, it didn't exactly feel *good*. And it certainly didn't come anywhere near the pleasure I felt when I just . . . helped myself.

"It was mostly just uncomfortable," I told Caroline, "and really, *really* fast."

Caroline laughed. "That gets better too."

The ancient waitress, who looked like she was about to collapse under the weight of the tray she was carrying, appeared next to us and set our breakfasts down. I busied myself pouring syrup on my pancakes and fiddling with the silverware until she left.

"Um, the main problem," I continued when I was sure she was out of earshot, "is that I don't think either of us knew what to do."

"Do?" Caroline echoed, unsure what I was asking.

"You know," I said. "I couldn't figure out what sorts of movements I was supposed to make."

Caroline looked puzzled. "I don't think you should choreograph it. And you know Jamie wouldn't want you to be fake with him."

"I know," I said. "You're right."

"Have you talked since you did it?"

"He called me right after he got home last night and again like two minutes after you called this morning."

"And?" She looked at me expectantly. "Are things cool?"

"Yeah." I grinned, feeling a blush spreading up to my cheeks. "He was really nice, and asked me about a million times if I was okay, and just seemed . . . grateful or something."

"Do you think you might like him now?" Caroline persisted. "As a boyfriend?"

I shook my head. "No way. We have an agreement. Nothing's going to change between us."

Caroline's eyes twinkled. "But think about it. Wouldn't it be kind of cool if it did?"

I shook my head. "Nope. Can't break the pact. If we thought of each other as anything more than friends, it could end up ruining our friendship, and neither of us wants to take that risk."

"Oh." For a split second Caroline looked disappointed. But then she grinned. "Are you at least going to do it again?"

I'd assumed, before I did it, that Jamie and I would be a one-shot deal. Now that the hard part was over with, it seemed a shame not to take advantage of the opportunity to . . . practice. It would be almost *wasteful*. Especially if Caroline was right and it really did feel better the second time.

Caroline was waiting for an answer, so I gave a little half shrug. "Maybe. Yeah."

She clapped. "Look at you and your exciting sex life!"

I looked at her, unable to stop the grin from spreading over my face.

"Hey, *I* have a *sex life*."

Caroline froze, staring over my shoulder. The waitress, our check in hand, had somehow materialized at our table.

She raised an eyebrow when she heard what I said.

I felt my face catch fire.

She slapped the check down without missing a beat.

"Enjoy it while you can, honey," she said, then shuffled back to the kitchen.

Sunday morning I woke up early. My parents and Hilly had gotten home late the night before.

Since there was no breakfast waiting, I figured my dad was probably down in his studio. I wandered in to say hi.

Dad's studio was my favorite place in the entire house. It took up half of the ground floor and had so many windows that it felt like a greenhouse, even in winter. The walls were lined with shelves and crammed with every kind of paint you could want, in more colors than were imaginable. Stacks of canvases were propped up against the far side of the room, and speakers were suspended in every corner to fill the room with music while you worked.

Even though the sun was barely up, Dad was already hard at work, wearing the splattered pajama pants and Rhode Island School of Design sweatshirt that were his uniform. He had two dozen puddles of paint on the big ceramic tray he used as an easel and was standing back from the canvas he was working on, squinting at the face of the woman he had painted.

He looked over at me when I came in and smiled. "I can't hear what she's trying to tell me," he said.

That was the sort of comment that used to make the

neighborhood kids tease me, but the better I got at painting myself, the more I understood what he meant.

"There's more to faces than what you can see on the outside," he once told me. "Unless you show what's inside, your painting won't succeed."

I looked at the picture. He was right—the woman he'd painted was beautiful, but flat—there was none of the life in her that made all his other paintings so special.

"Are you going to have to start over?" I asked.

He shook his head. "I think I'll give her a little more time. She deserves a chance to come around."

I smirked. "Don't we all?"

I walked over to the easel I'd set up in the sunniest corner of the room and looked at the painting *I* was working on. It was supposed to be a pop-art self-portrait, but in it, I looked more like a Japanimation action hero.

Apparently when I looked in a mirror, what I saw was Sailor Moon.

Dad came up behind me and looked at the painting over my shoulder. "You see? We have the same problem. We both name names."

"What do you mean?" I asked.

He pointed to the painting, his finger hovering over each part of the face. "You think 'eye,' and that's what you paint. Then you think 'nose' and paint a nose."

I had no idea what he meant. "How am I supposed to paint a face without eyes and noses?"

"By naming the part, you have a preconceived idea of what it's supposed to look like." He paused, seeing my confusion. "You paint exactly what you think you need to, instead of using your *feelings* to make the painting great."

He grabbed my tray and swept out the tubes of brown and beige oils I'd laid out into it. "Here—let's try something else. I want you to paint an *inner* self-portrait."

He led me over to the shelves of paint and started pulling down bright reds and purples and oranges. "Forget about form, forget about realism. Paint *you*. What's *inside* you."

Okay . . .

I grabbed a fresh canvas and retreated to my easel. I shut my eyes for a second, trying to see the image that wanted to come out. Then I squeezed daubs of the colors onto the palette.

Dad crossed to the CD player and slid in a disc. Classical music filled the studio—the "Danse Macabre"—a wild frenzy of violins and cello that was as volatile as the image I wanted to paint.

"Don't censor yourself!" Dad shouted to be heard over the music. "Open yourself to the process. Be honest. True art grows out of vulnerability. Don't think—create!"

I let the music swirling around me guide my brush to the

canvas. All the craziness of the past few weeks poured out of me. Jamie and Noah and sex and uncertainty and frustration and possibility—it all flowed from my brain to my hand to the painting.

Dad had apparently inspired himself with his words too. He was adding streaks of pink and gold to the shadows on the woman's face and humming along off-key to the music.

After a while I got so caught up in the art that I forgot he was even there. I lost track of time. The only thing on my mind was the movement of my brush, the colors, the clamor of the music. I didn't even see what I was painting until I was finished. Then I set my brush down and took a step back, gazing at my creation. Dark violets faded to a soft lavender and mingled with a narrow strip of pale green. It didn't look like me—it didn't even look like a person. But I liked it anyway. It looked the way I felt.

Dad turned the volume on the stereo down and came over to stand next to me.

"Marit! What's happened to you?"

I stopped, startled by the question. "H-how do you mean?" I asked nervously.

"You've really advanced," he said, examining the painting closely. "Even since the piece you did last week. Something inside you has changed."

Oh, crap. Could my dad somehow see what the picture was

about? He was going to ship me off to Catholic school before the paint was even dry!

"Huh," I answered, trying to look innocent. "I don't know. I mean, nothing's changed."

"You're using more complicated techniques, your composition is getting better—all in all, this piece shows a lot of maturity. You are really growing up!"

I smiled weakly and Dad slung his arm around my shoulders, giving me a squeeze.

"Just do me one favor," he said, planting a kiss on top of my head, "don't grow up too fast. I'm not ready to let go of my little girl."

I gazed up at him, and a feeling like sadness fluttered through me.

Part of me wanted him to know what was going on inside me . . . the same part that realized he never could know.

"Don't worry, Dad. I'm still your little girl," I told him.

Deep down, I hoped it was true.

14

At the crack of dawn Monday morning, my eyes flew open, the third day in a row where I woke up insanely early.

Maybe I was anxious about seeing Jamie for the first time since we did it. Because no matter how hard I tried, I couldn't fall back asleep.

I finally got up and headed to school early. As I walked along, I started wondering, every time I looked at Jamie now, would I picture what he looked like naked?

It was pretty amusing to think about until I realized that maybe he'd be picturing me naked too.

I was so preoccupied with the thought that I almost didn't hear Noah calling to me.

"Marit!"

I snapped out of my trance—a split second too late. I turned and walked straight into Mr. Rodriguez, the three-hundred-pound physics teacher.

I bounced off his stomach, lost my balance, and landed directly on my butt.

Mr. Rodriguez clamped a meaty hand on my arm to help me up. "Hey. You all right?" he asked.

"Yeah. Sorry," I mumbled. I heard a chorus of laughter coming from the athletic field and turned to look.

The lacrosse team was having an early practice, and Noah was with them, stretching out. He wasn't, however, the one laughing. Juliet Hammond and the rest of the Pradas were sitting on the sidelines. They had witnessed the entire incident and apparently found it the funniest moment of the century.

I wanted to slink away and pretend some other girl had just made a jackass of herself, but Noah called my name again, so I had no choice but to walk over.

"Hey. You okay?" he asked when I came up to him. "You're walking kind of funny."

My face flushed hot. Oh, dear God! I was stammering around for an excuse when Noah interrupted me.

"You really gave your ankle a wrench there," he said. "Are you sure you didn't sprain it?"

Ah. The ankle . . .

"It's okay," I told him. "I just twisted it a little."

Noah dropped to his knees and wrapped his fingers gently around it, carefully checking to see if it was sprained.

We're just friends, I reminded myself, ignoring the little quiver in my stomach. *Just friends. Just friends.*

I opened my eyes as Noah was getting back up.

"It doesn't feel like it's anything serious," he said. "If it's still hurting later, you might want to ice it."

"Cool, thanks," I said, flexing my foot experimentally. "So are you, like, a huge fan of *ER* or something?"

Noah laughed. "No, I get banged up so much playing lacrosse that I guess I've picked up a few things. Practice can get a little rough."

I eyed his soaked T-shirt and grass-stained shorts. He even had a smudge of dirt on his cheek. "Really?" I joked. "'Cause it kind of looks like you've been dogging it."

Noah looked startled, so I continued on in my Ms. Vandermeer voice. "This isn't a day spa, you know. You can't be afraid of a little sweat."

Noah glanced down at his clothes, then grinned. "I guess I *am* a little grungy."

"Here—" I reached out a finger and wiped the smudge off his cheek. His skin was warm. "That's better. Now you'd fit in anywhere."

Noah glanced around at his teammates, all of whom were as disheveled as he was. "You're the one who doesn't fit in.

Here—" Noah reached out his finger and put a smudge of mud on my cheek. "Perfect."

I laughed and wiped the smudge off with the back of my hand. I was the picture of nonchalance, if I did say so myself. This not-being-a-virgin thing was already working out for me.

Then Rick Fielding came jogging up to us.

"Dude, come on," he told Noah. "We're running wind sprints."

"On my way," Noah called.

Juliet peeled herself off the grass and walked over. "Hi, Rick," she said, ignoring me and Noah.

"Hi, babe." Rick grabbed Juliet around the waist and gave her a short but disgustingly graphic kiss.

Noah and I both tried not to stare, but it was kind of like watching a boa constrictor swallow a man's head. Hard to ignore.

"We have our first match next week," Noah told me. "You should come and watch."

I opened my mouth to answer, but Juliet, who had detached herself from Rick and was drying off her face, jumped in first.

"Forget it, Noah," she said. "Marit thinks she's too hip to have anything to do with Sterling after school."

"I do not," I said, glaring at her.

"Please." She rolled her eyes. "Name one single thing you've participated in."

I couldn't believe that she was actually making fun of me for this! I knew for a fact she didn't want me at her bake sales and volleyball tournaments.

"I *participate*," I said. "It just happens that most of my activities take place outside of school."

Juliet tossed her hair and put a perfectly manicured hand on Noah's arm. "She thinks we're *sheep*," she told him conspiratorially.

"I do not!" I protested.

At least, I didn't think *Noah* was a sheep. . . .

"Ease up, Juliet," Noah said gently. "If Marit doesn't want to come to my lacrosse game, she doesn't have to."

Now, I know I'm not supposed to be crushing on him. But seeing the way he shrugged Juliet's hand off his arm made my heart give a little leap.

"I would love to come to your game," I said sweetly.

"It's your funeral," Juliet told him, and then sashayed back to her friends.

"Nice girl," Noah snarked, watching her go.

I grinned at him, trying *so hard* not to get my hopes up.

Then the coach blew his whistle and waved the team over.

"I gotta go. See you in class?" Noah said.

I nodded. "Bye."

Noah turned and jogged back out onto the lacrosse field. I headed into school. . . .

So I'd have to sit through a lacrosse game, I thought. So what? Even if my friends thought I was totally insane, it would be worth it.

Jamie had a dentist appointment, so he wasn't in homeroom. But when I got to orchestra, he was waiting there, smiling.

"Hey," I said, hesitating. Was he going to want to kiss me hello or something?

But Jamie just said "hey" back, in a totally normal voice, then opened the door to the band room. "After you."

Uh-oh. I panicked again. Did *that* mean something, his holding the door? Wasn't that something a boyfriend would do?

I know it didn't seem like that big a deal, but if Jamie started acting all sweet and chivalrous, it would just be too weird.

I made it to my seat, then glanced back at Jamie, who was still holding the door for the three students who came in after me.

Okay. Maybe *I* was the one being weird.

We were starting today on a Mozart chamber piece that had some really tricky bow-work, so I slumped down in the sixth-chair seat and opened my violin case with a sigh.

Jamie came over a moment later. He narrowed his eyes at me, then sank down in the seventh chair without comment.

He pulled his own violin out of its case and started tuning up.

"Does this sound flat?" he asked me, tightening one of his strings and then playing a note.

I looked at him, mystified. "Depends on what note you were trying to play."

"Um, middle C?"

I leaned forward and tapped one of the trumpet players on her shoulder. "Can you play us a C?" I asked.

She did, and Jamie played his note again.

I couldn't hear any difference, but the trumpeter shuddered. "Dude, you're way sharp."

Jamie looked at me and shrugged, then started loosening the string.

"We are gifted in other ways," he said.

Mr. Murphy stepped up to the conductor's podium and tapped his baton, signaling us all to settle down and get ready to begin. Before we could launch into the opening notes of the piece, however, Jamie raised his hand and waved it around, making himself impossible to ignore.

Mr. Murphy sighed. "What is it, Jamie?" he asked.

Jamie cleared his throat. "I would like to challenge Marit for the sixth-chair position."

What?! I shot Jamie a dirty look, and he smirked at me. So much for being sweet and chivalrous!

Mr. Murphy sighed again. I remembered hearing that when he was younger, Mr. Murphy played for the Pittsburgh

Symphony. I wondered what cruel twist of fate had landed him here, in the third circle of musical hell.

"Jamie Lyons, you and Marit are both sixth chair," he explained. "You share that position."

"Nevertheless, I feel that my playing is such that I deserve a shot at *that seat*," Jamie continued, pointing at the chair I was sitting in.

"Marit, do you mind switching?" Mr. Murphy asked wearily.

I could see his hair growing grayer. I felt for him, I did. However . . .

"Actually? I do mind. Sorry," I said, then added under my breath, "since I'm clearly the better musician."

The rest of the band shifted impatiently in their seats.

The trumpet player who had helped us find the note earlier muttered, "Jesus *Christ*," loud enough for everyone to hear.

Mr. Murphy shut his eyes for a moment, then opened them. "Anyone who wishes to challenge for a chair may come in after school and do it then. Now"—Jamie was waving his hand around again, but Mr. Murphy ignored him—"let's play some Mozart!"

The rest of the orchestra started the piece. I turned to Jamie to complain, but he was very studiously examining the sheet music as he lifted his violin to his chin.

I picked up my instrument too, but before I could make

Pop!

a single sound, Jamie played a screeching note that was so off-key, the entire orchestra winced.

Instead of apologizing, Jamie shot me a gaping, wide-eyed look—as though *I* was the one who made the mistake.

"D-flat, Marit," Mr. Murphy scolded over the noise of the concerto. "Get it right."

I squinted at Jamie.

The boy was diabolical. And *hilarious*.

"Sorry," I mumbled, trying not to laugh.

We took the concerto from the top.

SCREEEE! Jamie did it again!

"Really, Marit!" he cried. Then he gazed at me pityingly, sad that they would let such an awful musician maul the works of Amadeus.

By the time we got all the way through the piece, Jamie had made six mistakes, all of which he blamed on me. I was laughing so hard I couldn't have played the right notes even if I knew how. And Mr. Murphy, I was fairly certain, was already planning his move back to Pittsburgh.

Mr. Murphy dismissed the class early and headed off to his office mumbling something about there not being enough Advil in the *universe.*

I put my violin carefully in its velvet-lined case and looked at Jamie.

"You really should practice more," he said solemnly.

"Jamie!" I scolded.

But he laughed and breezed out of the room.

I jumped up and scrambled after him, completely, thoroughly happy. Everything was going to be just fine. In fact, maybe for the first time in my life, everything was going right. I wasn't a virgin, Noah and I were becoming buds, and nothing had changed in my friendship with Jamie.

Senior year might just work out the way I hoped after all!

acrosse?!" Caroline said, her voice a combination of horror and disgust.

"Well, yeah," I said, unsure what she was getting so screechy about. "It's the first match of the season, and Noah asked me to come, so—"

"You aren't actually going to _go_, are you?" she interrupted. "You hate lacrosse. You hate _all_ sports."

Which actually was kind of funny, seeing as she was saying this to me from the downward dog position, which I was in too.

My mom always invites us to come to her yoga class before school, but this was the first time we had ever taken her up on it.

We should have stayed in bed.

Aury Wallington

Yoga is hard, boring, and *not* a good place to talk about boys. However—

"Well, of course I hate lacrosse, but I want to support Noah."

Caroline collapsed to the mat and looked at me, horrified. "Are you *joking*?"

"What? I thought you liked him."

"I do, I guess. As much as I could like *anybody* in a letter jacket. Only"—the instructor called out for the plank position, so we flipped onto our stomachs—"what about Jamie?"

"What about him?" I asked, trying unsuccessfully to lift my upper body off the mat.

"It just seems—*weird* that you'd go out with Noah while you and Jamie are—" She glanced over at my mom, who was planking a few feet away, then mouthed what looked like "knockin' boots."

"Noah and I are just friends," I said, checking to make sure my mom couldn't hear. "For that matter, *Jamie* and I are just friends. I'm not going out with Noah. I've totally come to terms with the fact that he doesn't like me that way."

My heart gave a little ache as I said the words.

"Thank God," Caroline said.

I glared at her. "And so what if he did? You know how much I liked him."

"I know." She touched my arm sympathetically, and I

146

realized she wasn't actually doing the plank at all, just lying on her stomach. "I just don't want to see anyone get their feelings hurt."

For some reason, this annoyed me.

"Caroline, no one—not me, not Noah, not Jamie—*no one* is going to get hurt!"

Caroline nodded, satisfied. "Good."

The instructor called out for the class to do the plow, so we turned onto our backs and tried to flip our legs over our heads. Caroline kicked her feet so wildly the instructor came hurrying over to help lift her legs into the right position.

I managed to get my legs upside down but then realized I was being smothered by my boobs, which were being squashed up against my lungs. I couldn't breathe, so before I suffocated, I flipped back down on the mat in child's pose—my favorite position by far, since it was almost like taking a little nap.

The second the instructor let go of her ankles, Caroline also gave up any pretense and rolled over onto the mat next to me.

"So, speaking of you and Jamie"—she nudged me with her elbow—"when are you guys planning to do it again?"

"Funny you should ask," I told her. "We're doing it tonight."

She gasped in mock shock. "You *dogs!*"

My parents were taking Hilly to meet with a new college

admissions strategist that afternoon, so Jamie and I were taking advantage of the empty house to "re-create the magic."

So to speak.

I winked saucily at Caroline. "Why do you think I wanted to come to yoga? *CosmoGirl* says guys like it when you're flexible."

She grinned, rubbing her hands together all businesslike. "Why didn't you say so? Let's get you back into that downward dog!"

That afternoon my family left the house at four o'clock. By 4:03, Jamie and I were doing it. Again.

To be honest, it still wasn't an earth-shattering experience. It didn't hurt, but it was over really fast, and aside from the initial excitement, I didn't really feel . . . anything.

There had to be something more. Didn't there?

Jamie rolled off me, lying back against my pillow and catching his breath.

Okay, now what? I wondered.

I supposed I could get up and get dressed, but I couldn't figure out how to do that without Jamie seeing me naked. I mean, *completely* naked.

Because the first time we did it, the room was dark. And yeah, I had gotten undressed in front of him just a few minutes earlier, but then we'd been so focused on what we were doing that the fact that we were both naked was kind of secondary.

If I got out of bed *now*, he would definitely be able to check out my body. And since the sunlight was streaming in through the windows, there pretty much wasn't anything he *wouldn't* see.

Which was just—yikes!

I was furtively looking around to see if my underwear was close enough to the bed that I could grab it and put it on without getting out from underneath the covers when Jamie lifted up the top of the sheet a little bit and peeked underneath.

"Jamie!" I shouted, turning red and clamping my arm down so he couldn't lift it up again.

"What?" he asked innocently.

"What do you think you're doing?! There's a reason we have blankets, you know."

"Yeah, but—what's the point of experience if you can't see what you're experienced with?"

"That makes no sense," I told him.

"Look, I'm sorry," he said with a grin. "But if I actually have a chance to see what a girl looks like naked, I've gotta take it."

I frowned. "Well, you could have warned me first."

"Why, so you could suck in your stomach?" Jamie teased.

Well, yeah.

"Look, the point is—" I stopped, trying to think up my point. Before I could come up with anything, Jamie gave me a sidelong glance.

"You wanna look too?"

Oh my God. "No." I shook my head. "I couldn't."

"Well, you *could*," Jamie said, "if you wanted to."

"Really?" I asked, tempted but shy.

Instead of answering, Jamie lifted the sheet back up, high enough for me to see under.

I took a deep breath, daring myself. Then I peeked. First with just one eye, then the other.

I wasn't sure what I was expecting. I guess I thought it would be monstrous, like something you'd see on the Internet. Turns out it didn't look that way. In fact, it was smaller than I imagined.

Naturally, I didn't say that to Jamie.

"Do you, uh, want to touch it?" he asked.

Why not? I thought. After all, I'd touched it before. I was an old pro at touching it.

I reached my fingers toward it. And it *twitched*.

"Jeez!" I snatched my hand away.

"Sorry." Jamie smirked. "It, uh, does that."

I cleared my throat. "Maybe we should just—get dressed."

Jamie nodded. "Baby steps."

So I went first and got out of bed. And even though I wasn't really shy anymore . . . the truth was, I have never gotten dressed that fast in my life!

16

My high school is trying to kill me.

More specifically, the lunch ladies are trying to kill off everyone in second period. I mean, why else would they serve curried lentil loaf at 9 a.m?

Eating something that disgusting, that early, would be total suicide. Or rather, legume-icide.

I took one bite and—

"God, this is awful!" I cried.

Everyone at my table dropped their forks, giving me pitying glances. *They* had wisely chosen salads.

I tried to wipe my tongue off with my napkin, but it was no use.

"It's like the flavor has seared itself into my brain!" I told Caroline. "I can't get rid of it!"

Nina patted my back. "Why don't you go brush your teeth?"

I nodded. "Good idea."

I grabbed a hall pass from the lunchroom monitor and swiped my toothbrush from my locker. I ducked into the nearest girls' room, fighting the urge to vomit.

As fate would have it, there was someone retching in the bathroom already.

"Lunch ladies got you too?" I asked, calling over the door of the stall.

"Hand me a paper towel," the girl croaked from the other side.

I pulled a wad of towels from the dispenser and walked over to the stall. The door was open and Dana, the pregnant girl from my gym class, was kneeling on the floor.

She was gripping the porcelain bowl with both hands, and her head rested against the toilet paper dispenser.

It was the saddest thing I'd ever seen.

Gingerly I handed her the towels. "Um, are you okay? Do you want me to go get the nurse?"

Dana shook her head. "I'll be fine in a second."

She wiped her mouth and hands with the paper towels, then tossed them into the toilet.

"Oh—you shouldn't flush those," I said, "they'll ruin the—"

She flushed.

"—pipes," I finished lamely.

Pop!

Dana struggled to her feet as I hovered helpfully behind her. I felt like I should offer her a hand, but I didn't want to touch any part of her that might have come into contact with vomit. She walked over to the sink and started rinsing her mouth.

"So, uh, you ate the lentil loaf too?" I asked.

Dana shot me a look that clearly said I was the stupidest person she'd ever spoken to.

"It's morning sickness," she snapped.

Right. Hadn't really thought about that.

I started digging through my purse for a peace offering. A stick of gum or maybe a breath mint. Alas, I came up empty.

I held out my mini-tube of toothpaste.

"Want some?"

Dana shook her head. "Gag me." She started to brush past me, but—

"Uh, you have some vomit on your shirt," I pointed out.

Dana whirled around . . . and her eyes filled up with tears.

"Oh God. I'm sorry," I said. "I just thought, I'd want someone to tell *me* if I—"

"It's not that. I'm glad you said something," Dana sobbed. "It's just—being pregnant sucks."

I had no doubt.

She ducked down to the sink to splash some water on her shirt. I didn't know what to say next, so I tried to change the subject. "Um, do you have a name picked out yet?"

Okay, that wasn't exactly a brand-new subject, but at least it seemed positive.

She smiled. "Michael Junior."

"Junior?" I repeated, surprised.

Dana gave me an amused look in the mirror. "Yes, junior. What? You think I don't know who the father is?"

I gulped. Dana's skankiness was the stuff of legend, so I had assumed that with all the millions of guys she slept with, maybe she had lost track of exactly whose baby it was.

"I'm sorry. I didn't mean—" I started to apologize, but she cut me off.

"I've only been with one guy. So I think chances are pretty good he's the one."

"One guy?" I asked.

"Yes. My fiancé, Michael. He's the only one."

"I am sorry," I told her, completely sincere. "It's just—"

"You heard all those rumors about me and believed them?" Dana finished.

"Yeah," I confessed, feeling sheepish.

"Look, I admit, I fooled around a *lot,*" she said. "But I never, ever went all the way. Until *this.*"

God. Pregnant the first time she did it . . .

She really *was* an after-school special. I found myself looking at Dana in a whole different light.

She straightened up and dried off her shirt as best she could. Then she threw away the paper towels and gave herself a small smile in the mirror. "How do I look?"

I took in her straggly hair, vomit-stained shirt, and baggy pants and decided if there was ever a time for charity, or a worthy recipient, this was it.

"Are you kidding?" I told her. "You're *glowing*."

She smiled then, and she actually did glow a little.

She waited for me while I brushed my teeth, and we headed back to the cafeteria together.

Caroline, Jamie, and I had plans to see a movie that afternoon after school. Caroline's mom wanted her to swing by her house first, though, so Jamie and I went on to my house to wait.

There was no one else home, and when we went inside, Jamie sat down on the couch and held a hand out to me.

"C'mere."

I didn't budge.

"Caroline's going to be here any minute," I told him. "We don't have time to fool around."

I didn't add that talking to Dana that morning had freaked me out. I didn't want him to so much as *look at me* without using protection.

Jamie grinned and shook his head. "No. It's just—I got you something."

"A present?" I chirped.

I am a total sucker for presents.

I sat down next to him, and he pulled a CD case out of his backpack. He'd made the cover himself, a patchwork of images from different magazines. A field of flowers, a construction site, a dog in a raincoat . . .

Somehow he'd gotten the yellow parts of the pictures to line up and overlap so that when you looked at the collage from a distance, the overlapping pieces spelled out my name.

"Wow! This is great," I told him. "What songs are on it?"

"Put it on and see."

I walked over to the stereo and slipped it in. The cheesy intro for Journey's "Open Arms" started.

I gave Jamie a quizzical look.

"This is the song that was playing on the radio in your kitchen when we decided we were going to—you know."

"Really? I didn't realize that!" I hit skip, and the next song came on, Fall Out Boy's "Sugar We're Going Down."

"We were listening to this album when I helped you put together your bookshelves," I remembered.

Jamie nodded. "When, I believe, the subject first came up."

I hit skip again. The Mozart concerto we were butchering in orchestra was next.

"So *that's* what this piece is supposed to sound like," I said.

Jamie laughed. "Are you kidding? We're way better than those hacks at the London Philharmonic."

I hit fast-forward again, and "Let's Stay Together" came on. I gasped. "Jamie, do you realize what this is?"

"What?" he said softly.

"It's a sex sound track!" I stage-whispered. "What if someone found this?"

He laughed. "I think our reputations will be safe."

The chorus of the song started, my favorite part, and I couldn't help myself from joining in.

"Whether . . . times are good or bad, happy or sad . . ."

I smiled. This was just like Jamie, marking an occasion with a mix tape. A few months ago, when Caroline broke up with the latest sap to fall for her, Jamie made a mix called "Songs for the Dumped." Ironically, it was filled with feel-good, super-cheesy pop. It had been the sound track to our summer.

As Al continued to sing, Jamie gave me a funny little smile. He walked up to me, holding out a hand.

"Want to dance?"

My mouth dropped open.

Since I was so much taller than all the boys at Sterling, I considered Jamie my fallback guy whenever we were forced to attend a school mixer.

But over all these years, no matter how much I begged, Jamie never agreed to actually dance with me.

"Really?" I asked.

"Really," he said, and pulled me into his arms.

He swayed us around the living room, his hands holding me close. It was sweet. So amazingly sweet. I felt safe with Jamie.

But I couldn't help wishing . . . wishing I had someone else to dance with.

A strand of Jamie's hair was brushing softly against my cheek, and he clutched me tighter. He sighed, barely a breath, really, almost too soft to hear.

My heart gave a little twist. I gently broke away.

"What?" he asked, confused and blinking, as if he'd just woken up from a nap.

"You know what," I teased him. "*That* is a song made for getting a girl's clothes off."

"That wasn't what I was trying to do at all," he protested, but I hit the stop button on the stereo and the music shut off.

I put the CD back in its case and tilted my face up to Jamie's. "I love the mix tape, though. Thanks for making it for me." I gave him a little peck on the lips.

"Sure," he said, still looking sort of fuzzy.

The doorbell rang, and a second later Caroline burst into the room.

"Help, you guys," she wailed, "I need to be around sanity."

She flopped down on the couch.

"Parents behaving badly?" Jamie asked, sitting next to her and throwing an arm across her shoulders.

Caroline nodded.

"What did they do now?" I asked, taking a place on her other side. Her shoulders were already taken, so I draped my legs across her lap.

She laughed and pushed them off.

"My mom is so nuts. She packed up all my dad's clothes. She says she's mailing them to his parents' house! She told me to call my grandma to make sure she had the right zip code."

Typical Emerson family dysfunction.

"I bet she'll calm down," I said. "There's no way she'll actually go through with taking them to the post office."

"You're probably right," Caroline agreed. "She wouldn't want to spend all that money on postage when she could use it to get a manicure or something."

"Poor Caro," Jamie said. Then he bolted upright. "Wait! I know something that'll cheer you up. There just so happens to be a revival playing at Cinema Classics that'll blow you away!"

"Is it *Pretty in Pink*?" Caroline guessed, perking up.

He rolled his eyes. "No. But it *is* one of the definitive films of contemporary cinema."

"*Pretty in Pink* is definitive," Caroline insisted.

"So, what obscure masterpiece are you going to make us watch instead?" I asked.

A huge smile spread across Jamie's face. "Today we're going to see something really special. *Ladri di biciclette!*"

Caroline and I looked at each other and groaned.

"*The Bicycle Thief?*" I asked. "We've seen that a million times."

"Not its original version, we haven't," Jamie said, excited.

"What's so special about the original version?" I asked.

"No subtitles." This seemed to make Jamie even happier. "It'll be a completely authentic experience."

"Yeah, one you'll have to enjoy alone," Caroline said. "Because there is *just no way* I can sit through that movie again."

"Me neither," I said.

"You guys are crazy," Jamie protested. "It's only one of the most formative pictures in filmmaking history."

"Yeah, but don't you think it's a little . . . cliché?" Caroline asked.

Jamie blinked at her, affronted. "How do you mean?"

"Pretentious film geek obsessed with *The Bicycle Thief* . . . ?" she teased.

"First of all," Jamie said, "I'm not pretentious. I'm not obsessed, and I'm certainly not a geek."

Caroline and I exchanged a glance—neither of us was going to touch that one.

"Let's vote," I suggested. "All in favor of *The Bike Thief?*"

Jamie winced at my shorthand but raised his hand.

"Okay, that's . . . one," I counted. "All in favor of *Pretty in Pink?*"

Caroline and I both raised our hands.

"It isn't even playing at a theater," Jamie complained. "We'd have to watch it on DVD."

"Then aren't we in luck," I said, "because I just so happen to have a copy right in the next room."

Jamie groaned, so Caroline threw an arm around his neck, putting him in a headlock.

"Tell you what," she joked, "if you watch this with us, Marit will have sex with you again!"

"Hey!" I protested, but Jamie was already racing into the next room, searching for the disc. Caroline was right behind him, cracking up.

I had no choice but to laugh and follow.

17

The next Friday was the day of the first lacrosse match. I wasn't sure what a person wore to watch lacrosse, but I wanted to look both athletic and sexy—neither of which came naturally.

I decided on vintage jeans and a black fitted shirt that was a little tight across the boobs but that I felt completely comfortable in.

The match was being held on the far athletic fields, past the football field, which was a good ten-minute hike from school. By the time I got there, I was amazed to discover that the bleachers were nearly full!

Hmph. Who knew that so many people cared so much about lacrosse?

We were playing a team from Rye, New York. I congratulated

myself for knowing enough to not sit on the bleachers on that side of the field, even though there were a lot more vacant seats to choose from.

Sterling's side was pretty dismal pickings, so I looked for a seat not too close to the front, that wasn't directly next to anyone I actively hated.

I ended up squeezing into a spot about a third of the way up, next to a couple of guys who looked like they probably were star players twenty years ago.

I thought about asking them if they were alumni, but the thought was just too depressing. God help me if, when I'm forty, I'm still reliving the glory days at good ol' Sterling Prep.

I smiled, thinking that given my current level of extracurricular involvement, the only way I could actively cling to high school would be to eat lunch at 9 a.m. and mispronounce *schwierigkeit*.

Out on the field, the cheerleaders started hollering to get everyone revved up for the game. Then the marching band— which, as a violinist, I was mercifully excused from—played a little peppy Sousa tune as the players ran out onto the field.

Right away I spotted Noah. He looked so good in his uniform that I had to whisper, "We're just friends, we're just friends," like a mantra until I could breathe normally again.

The players were headed to the bench on the sidelines, but

before he sat down, Noah scanned the bleachers. I gave him a little wave, and he grinned and waved back.

"Just friends!" I singsonged as I waggled my fingers. The guy next to me stared in alarm, then moved down a seat.

Why hadn't I ever realized how much fun watching lacrosse could be?

In the end, our team won the game, and there was so much hooting and jumping up and down that I didn't think I'd ever find Noah in all the commotion. But by the time he came out of the locker room, in a clean shirt with his hair still wet, most of the crowd had gone home.

Juliet and Emberly pulled up outside the locker room in Juliet's tacky white SUV. Apparently the rest of the team was going to Pizza Hut to celebrate, and a bunch of the players piled into her car.

"Noah, you coming?" Rick Fielding called as he took over the driver's seat.

I cringed, but Noah just waved them away. "See you guys tomorrow," he called back. Then he smiled down at me.

"I've had enough of them for one day," he said, leading me to his car. "Let's go somewhere without them around, acting like idiots."

I smiled back at him. "This will be a new experience for us. No jocks and absolutely no reason to speak German."

"Vorzüglich!" he answered.

I shot him a look. He pretended to cough. "Sorry. Just had to get it out of my system."

"No problem," I said, and followed him out to the parking lot.

We ended up having dinner at an odd little restaurant called Kiev. Jamie, Caroline, and I had driven past it a zillion times but had never even considered going inside.

I wondered how Noah had found it.

Inside, the decor was a strange mix of country charm and post-industrial utility—cheery gingham tablecloths over fold-out card tables, framed black-and-white Weegee prints of Depression-era workers hanging next to needlepoint kittens, heavy, beautiful china plates, and flimsy aluminum forks.

But candles flickered on every table, and wild gypsy music swirled out of the speakers. The waitress was the smiliest person I'd ever seen, and when she set down our meal, huge platters of pierogies and goulash, I was an instant convert.

"So," Noah said, "how'd you like the game?"

"Oh, it wasn't nearly as boring as I thought it would be," I blurted.

Noah laughed and grabbed at the imaginary knife I had just plunged into his chest, but I waved my hands for him to let me explain.

"You don't understand—I am the world's worst fan," I said. "I hate to watch sports, hate to play sports, hate everything *about* sports." I leaned forward conspiratorially. "So you have to realize what a *huge* compliment it was for me just to come to your game."

"I am overwhelmed by your generosity," Noah teased. "And you weren't even *that bored*!"

"Well, there was one thing on the field that I thought was pretty fun to watch," I admitted.

"Yeah, that Sterling screech owl is a riot," Noah agreed.

I poked him playfully with my fork, then helped myself to another pierogi.

"Seriously, though, I was really surprised at how much fun I had," I admitted.

"So I can expect to see you at the next game?" he asked.

I smirked. "Let's not get carried away."

"Okay," he said, his eyes smoldering. "But for the record, I'd really like for you to be there."

My heart gave a heavy thump in my chest.

Noah took a sip of water, then leaned back in his chair. "So, if you don't like sports, what do you like?"

"I like to paint," I told him. "My dad's an artist—that's what I want to be too."

"Cool," Noah said. "What kind of things do you paint?"

"Mostly abstracts, although sometimes I don't mean for them to be abstract—they just come out that way."

Noah smiled. "I bet they're amazing. Can I see them some-time?"

"Sure," I told him.

Then, out of the blue, his eyes lit up.

"Wait, I have the best idea," he said, positively beaming. "You should volunteer to paint the sets for *Guys and Dolls*!"

Oh, dear Lord. I could only imagine what Caroline and Jamie would say about that.

"Actually? My dad doesn't want me, uh, deviating from the stylistic form I'm exploring."

It wasn't entirely a lie—my dad thought our school's art teacher, Mrs. Lefferts, was crass and had no "eye." He wouldn't let me take any art classes at Sterling.

Which was totally fine with me.

"Oh." Noah looked disappointed. "I thought it would have been fun for us to do something *together*."

Together? I thought. *Like a couple?*

I hushed the mischievous voice inside me.

"Did you get a part?" I asked.

"Did I?" The beaming smile reappeared on Noah's face. "I got Sky Masterson! The lead!"

"Wow! Congratulations," I told him. "You must be really good."

"Honestly?" he said. "I think I got the part because I was the only one there who could sight-read music."

"I can sight-read," I said. "When I first started violin, our teacher made everyone learn. Of course, I can't *play* the notes, but I can read what they are."

"Well, if you don't want to paint sets, maybe you could join the cast. Even if you're just in the chorus or something, it'd be a blast."

"Yeah, I don't think so," I told him.

"Stage fright?" he asked.

"No, I just don't enjoy that sort of"—*pointless, phony, rah-rah Sterling*—"thing."

Noah shook his head, amused. "You're not going to make this easy for me, are you?"

I frowned. "How do you mean?"

He leaned forward, put his hand on mine. It felt like my arm was on fire.

"It's just—I like being with you, Marit," he said softly. "You're funny, you're smart. And you're the only person I've really connected with since I've been here. It was hard for me, moving to New York, leaving my mom back in Texas. But hanging out with you is making it easier."

He paused. "I'm trying to find ways to be around you. You know, without any pressure. . . ."

By now my heart was clanging in my chest.

"I—I can't join the play," I told him. "But I'll come and watch you."

Pop!

Noah smiled and let go of my hand. "Okay. It's a date."

A little perspective and clarity was definitely in order: this morning, when I'd asked my mom if she'd take me to the mall to buy new socks, she'd said, "It's a date."

But something inside me knew that this was not like that at all. It seemed, from what he was saying, that Noah liked me as *way* more than a friend. That maybe, he could still see things working out between us.

Which meant one thing—

I really, *really* had to stop doing it with Jamie.

Because sleeping with one guy when you were trying to get something started with another? Ranked right up there on the Top Ten Tackiest Ways to Ruin a Friendship.

Yes, I decided, I'd end things with Jamie tomorrow. And then I'd be free to follow *this* road wherever it led.

18

T ruth time: I didn't end things with Jamie.
I had sex with him instead.

I had called Caroline on Saturday morning so she could help me figure out exactly what to say to him. But her mom answered the phone and said, "She's with her father," in such an ominous tone that I was afraid to leave a message.

I knew I'd have to figure out the right words on my own.

I was pretty sure that no matter what I said, Jamie would be like, "Whatever," since, of course, we had a pact—and remained nothing more than best friends.

But when I went over to his house after lunch, before I had time to say anything more than "hi," he wrapped his arms around my waist and started kissing me.

"Jamie!" I whispered, pushing him away. "What are you doing?"

"What does it feel like?" he asked, moving in again.

"Wait—stop," I told him, struggling to form words. "We're—we're going to get caught."

"No, we're not," he said, grinning and pulling me closer.

"But your parents—" I said, and Jamie shook his head delightedly.

"They're *out*. For the *entire day*."

"Really?"

I couldn't believe it. Jamie's parents are ancient. They rarely ever leave the house, so Jamie never has the house to himself.

"It's true," he said. "Here, I'll show you." He took my arm and led me over to the wide staircase.

"Mom! Dad!" he shouted, loud enough for the whole house to hear. "Marit's here and we're going to have hot monkey sex in my room!"

He cupped a hand around his ear. "I don't hear the thump of their bodies dropping dead of shock, do you?"

I shook my head, mute.

"So, I guess the place is ours!" He started to pull me up the stairs.

"No, Jamie." I stopped him. "Here's the thing—I'm not having monkey sex—"

"Aw, please?" he begged. "This may be the only shot I get at defiling my bedroom."

"No, I—"

He moved behind me and danced around, making little "hoo-hoo" ape noises in my ear.

"Can't we at least have chimpanzee sex?" he asked.

"Jamie, no. You—"

"Baboon sex?" he asked, nuzzling my neck.

"Uh, no." I struggled to remain serious. But I could feel a smile creeping up on my face.

"How 'bout gorilla sex?" Jamie asked, turning me around to face him. "They're big, but they're gentle—"

Then all at once, he was kissing me again.

By now Jamie was good at the kissing part. He really knew what I liked.

I wondered, did I really want to give this up for *just the chance* of something with Noah?

Yes, I decided. Yes, I did. That was the point of this whole arrangement to begin with.

"Jamie," I began, stepping away from him. "Please. We need to talk."

Jamie's smile faded. His expression grew serious. "Okay. What's wrong?"

I took a deep breath.

"This has been good," I told him. "I mean, things have basically been okay, but I think—I think it's time for us to reconsider our arrangement."

Jamie looked puzzled. Which was weird. But, I guess, better than hurt or angry.

"What do you mean, basically?" he asked.

Now I was puzzled. "I mean, I think maybe we should stop—"

"No, no, no," he cut me off. "You said it's 'basically' been good. What do you mean?"

Um. "I don't know, I just meant that it's good. It never hurts anymore and . . . you know. It's fine."

"Fine?" Jamie shut his eyes for a second. "So, it's only been 'fine' for you?"

"Hasn't it been fine for you?" I asked.

Jamie let out a little barking laugh. "Marit. It's been amazing. Mind-blowing. Life-changing. Not just *'fine.'*"

Oh.

"Jamie. I didn't mean—"

"I see what's going on here." Jamie folded his arms and nodded in bitter realization. "I suck in bed."

"What?" I yelped.

"Here I thought we were having this incredible experience, and the whole time you were gritting your teeth and thinking about—I don't know, what *were* you thinking about? Calculus homework? What to have for dinner? Who was going to be this season's Apprentice?"

"Jamie," I told him. "You're making a big deal out of nothing. It was *fi*—great, I mean, it was great and I liked it, but I just never—you know."

"Oh my God." Jamie buried his face in his hands. "It's true. I *do* suck in bed!"

"No! It's not your fault," I reassured him. "It just . . . doesn't always happen for girls."

Jamie lifted his head and looked at me, thinking about this. "But sometimes it *does*."

I shrugged. "Yeah. I mean, I guess so."

He clapped, rubbed his hands together. "Marit, you've got to give me another shot."

"Jamie—"

"I'm serious! You can't tell me something like that and not give me a chance to do it right."

"I don't think—" I started, but he cut me off again.

"Marit. It can't end like this. I need to know that I'm not a total loser. I mean, how am I supposed to have any kind of confidence if I can't . . . you know."

He fixed me in his gaze, all seriousness. "Come on. If you never . . . got the full experience, then we might as well have not had sex in the first place. Right?"

I studied him for a moment.

Actually? I thought. *He kind of has a point.*

"One more shot?" I repeated.

He nodded. "That's all I ask."

I turned and walked up the stairs to his room.

Jamie ran his fingertips down my body, then followed them with his lips.

My brain was swirling—I was trying really hard to remember exactly what was happening, how it felt, but I couldn't hang on to a thought, couldn't keep anything in my head for more than an instant before it swirled away.

Something was building inside me, a ripple that started small but was getting bigger and bigger.

I couldn't get my mind around what was happening because I just wanted Jamie to—to keep doing *that*, only a little bit harder.

I worried that I was taking too long, worried that he'd stop, but he didn't. The ripple became a wave, and I couldn't catch my breath, couldn't keep my eyes open, couldn't control myself.

The feeling grew, and all at once I was exploding into a million pieces, being swept off the bed and spiraling away into the universe. I saw bright popping starbursts of light, couldn't breathe or talk or form thoughts.

It was a million times better than anything I'd ever felt by myself.

I don't know if I made noise, or moved my arms, or any of the other things I always paid attention to before—I couldn't concentrate on anything except the *feeling*.

My world was literally rocked, and then it was over and I was lying in Jamie's arms.

I lay there, breathing hard, completely overwhelmed by what had just happened.

Jamie was watching me with a funny smile on his face. If anything, I'd say he looked *proud*.

"Are you okay?" he asked.

I nodded. "That was—it was—"

"Amazing," Jamie said, holding me tightly. "Are you sure you—you know?"

"Definitely."

"Good."

I lay there in his arms for a few minutes, then yawned and stretched. "You want to get up and see about a snack?"

But Jamie shook his head. "Not yet," he said, holding me tighter. "Let's stay like this a little longer."

I shut my eyes and snuggled up closer.

Jamie sighed contentedly. "Remember this," he murmured in my ear. "This is what they're talking about. This is how it's supposed to be."

I smiled, imagining how it *could* be, for either of us, with someone we really loved.

Later that afternoon Jamie and I were fully dressed again, sitting at his kitchen table doing our homework as if nothing had happened.

Except every time I opened my mouth, Jamie would give me this *grin*, like he was remembering the things we just did and couldn't believe how lucky we were to have done them.

"You guys?" Caroline called softly, letting herself in Jamie's front door.

I glanced up.

Caroline's nose was beet red and her eyes were puffy and swollen—she looked like she'd been crying for hours.

"Oh my God, what happened to you?" I asked as Jamie and I jumped up from the table.

"M-my parents," she stuttered, her eyes filling with fresh tears.

"What about them?" Jamie prodded.

"My parents are getting divorced," she cried.

"Oh no," I said.

I folded Caroline into my arms. Jamie ran to fetch her a glass of water. When she had calmed down a little, we sat down next to her on the couch.

"I was supposed to stay at my dad's the whole weekend,"

she started, "but when my mom dropped me off, he wasn't home yet, so I got on his computer to check my e-mail—"

"Oh my God, you didn't find porn, did you?" Jamie asked.

I smacked him on the arm. "God, shut up. Of course she didn't." Then I turned to Caroline. "You didn't—did you?"

"No, but when I turned the computer on, his profile from match.com was up on the screen! He's, like, dating other people!"

"Jeez," Jamie said.

"I can't believe it," I muttered.

"I mean, I knew my parents were lunatics and all, but I thought they were trying to work things out. I had no idea things were *this* bad."

I gave Caroline a reassuring pat on her leg. "Maybe he was just goofing around when he filled it out—like we did that one time."

Caroline sniffled some more. Then shook her head. "While I was looking at the screen, my mom came in because she forgot she wanted to talk to my dad about something. When she saw what was there, she went ballistic."

"Ouch."

"Yeah. So she was waiting there when he got home, and they went outside, and when he came back in an hour later, my father told me that it's over for good, and they're getting divorced."

"Oh, Caro," I whispered.

She gulped at the water Jamie had given her, then straightened up, swiping away any lingering tears with the back of her hand.

"It's okay," she said in a more normal tone of voice. "I knew it was bound to happen one day. They never loved each other. I don't know why they got involved to begin with. It was just a recipe for disaster."

We were quiet for a moment. I rubbed Caroline's back and stared at the carpet, feeling vaguely uncomfortable.

"Okay, enough weeping and moaning." Caroline finally broke the silence. "I don't want to think about it any more today. What do you guys feel like doing?"

Jamie raised his hand. "I feel like kicking your butt at Monopoly."

"You could *try* . . ." Caroline told him.

"Thimble in the hou-ouse!" I singsonged, trying to sound like a badass.

"Oh, you're on," Caroline said. "But I want to be the thimble."

"No fair," I argued. "The thimble is the coolest piece, and I already called it."

"Hey, I'm the child of a broken home," Caroline said.

I looked at Jamie. "Why do I have the feeling we're going to be hearing a lot of that from now on?"

We hung out all afternoon, Caroline trouncing us, as promised, in the end.

Jamie offered to give us a ride home, but Caroline said she felt like some fresh air, so I walked with her the half mile back to our street.

"Are you sure you're okay?" I asked her.

She shook her head. "I will be. But let's not talk about it."

"Okay."

We walked along for a few steps, then her eyes lit up. "Oh! You never told me about the lacrosse game. How was it? Totally barbaric and awful?"

"Actually, it wasn't bad," I admitted. "And the best part is— I think I still have a chance with Noah!"

Caroline stopped. "What?"

"I know! Isn't it great—I could still have a boyfriend for senior year!"

I was expecting Caroline to start gushing, but her face darkened.

"I don't believe you," she snapped.

I looked at her, confused. "What?"

"You can't treat Jamie this way."

I frowned. "What way?"

"You can't just sleep with him and then go have sex with Noah right in his face."

My mouth fell open in shock. "I didn't sleep with Noah in Jamie's face. I didn't sleep with Noah at all! I didn't even kiss him," I reminded her. "And anyway, the whole *point* of me and

Jamie hooking up was so I'd be able to find a real boyfriend, remember?"

"And how's Jamie supposed to feel when that happens?"

"Uh, happy for me? Like *you* should be?" I said, wounded.

Caroline's eyes narrowed. "You need to be careful, Marit. This could blow up in your face. You could lose Jamie as a friend. And you don't want that."

"Oh my God, what are you *talking* about?" I asked. "Jamie's not going to be upset if I start seeing someone. We have an understanding."

"Yeah, well, maybe Jamie understands, but I don't," Caroline snapped.

At that moment I didn't think it mattered if Caroline understood or not. She wasn't the one I was sleeping with. But after the weekend she'd had, I figured I should probably cut her some slack and explain again.

"Jamie and I aren't *dating*. He doesn't think of me as his *girl*friend; he thinks of me as his *friend*friend, and that's it. We've got everything under control."

"I don't think this is something you *can* control," Caroline said. "Sex changes things. It has to."

I stared at her, unsure if I wanted to yell at her or to burst into tears. "Look, I'm ending things with Jamie. And if something serious develops with Noah, I'll make sure Jamie doesn't get hurt."

Caroline didn't answer, and we walked the last block to our houses in silence. When we reached the spot where our driveways touched, we stopped.

"Do you want to come have dinner with us?" I asked. She shook her head.

"No. I should make sure my mom's okay."

She started to walk away, but I touched her arm. "Are you mad at me?" I asked, still confused about what had happened.

She sighed and shook her head again. "No. I'm not mad. I'm just . . ." She trailed off, then shrugged. "Just promise you'll let Jamie down easy?"

"Of course."

Caroline finally smiled. "Good." Then she turned and walked up the driveway to her house.

19

Jamie came home with me after school on Monday to work on our chemistry homework. We came in through the kitchen door and found my dad there, surrounded by what looked like every single dish and pan we owned.

Jamie and I exchanged a look. This much cooking could mean only one thing—something major was going on with my dad's paintings.

"Mr. Anders," Jamie joked, "no one has to get hurt here. Just put the cookware down and back away slowly. . . ."

My father looked up. "Oh. Hi, kids," he greeted us.

"Dad," I said cautiously. "Something wrong?"

"Nope," he said cheerfully, a funny look on his face. "Just making paella."

"And the occasion would be . . ." I led him.

He broke into a huge grin. "Oh, just thought we'd cele-brate the fact that one of my paintings is being included in the opening night show at the Chelsea Gallery."

"Wow! Congratulations!" Jamie said.

I gave my dad a big hug. The opening of any new gallery was a huge event, and Dad had been campaigning to be included in this show for weeks.

"No big deal," he said, completely offhandedly, but when he turned toward us, I could see the massive grin on his face.

"When is the opening?" I asked.

"This Saturday."

"Fantastic," Jamie said, then turned to me. "I bet a night in the city would really cheer Caroline up."

"We'll ask her, but I don't know if she'll want to go," I said, worried. "I already offered to go shopping this weekend, but she said she didn't want to leave the house—in case her mom needed her."

"Miss Caroline is going through a rough time right now," Dad said. "I can understand if she wants to spend a couple of weekends at home. But I bet if you called and told her I was making paella, that'd get her over here quick."

He was right. Caroline's mom was working late, so Caroline agreed to come to dinner. She appeared at the back door thirty seconds later.

Jamie and I needed to finish our homework, so since

Caroline doesn't take chemistry, my dad put her to work in the kitchen, scrubbing the mussels he was putting in the paella.

We had only been at it an hour when I found my mind wandering. I looked down at my notebook and realized that I had been doodling Noah's name in the margins.

Yikes!

I covered my scribbles with my hand and shot a glance over at Jamie. His nose was buried in his book.

I turned the page. If this wasn't a sign, I wasn't sure what was. Maybe I should let Jamie know where things were going with Noah. Maybe I should tell him *right now*.

I opened my mouth to speak.

"Shhh! Studying," Jamie said, still concentrating on his book.

I blinked in surprise. How did he know I was about to say something? Did he have ESP?

I heard Caroline cackling in the kitchen, her laugh loud and unapologetic. Then she and my father started singing—a song we learned in fifth grade.

"Cockles and muscles alive alive-ooooo!" they warbled off tune.

Jamie smiled into his book and continued reading.

I stared at his face, and my heart swelled.

I did love Jamie, I realized. We were so close, it was almost as if we were parts of the same whole. I couldn't begin to imagine my life without him. . . .

But the way I loved Jamie wasn't any different than the way I loved Caroline or even Hilly. They were *all* a part of me.

What I needed was something different . . . something more.

I hated having secrets from Jamie. There was so much I wanted to tell him, but . . .

But right now Caroline was laughing with my dad and Jamie was sitting next to me so calm, so steady.

It was a perfect moment. I couldn't ruin it.

I turned back to my book, and as I read the same paragraph for the third time in a row, I sensed Jamie looking up.

"Shhh!" I told him. "Studying."

He gave a low chuckle and flipped to the next chapter.

The next night I was in my room, adding a painting of a heron to my closet mural, when the phone rang.

My mom called up the stairs that it was for me, so I set down my brush and grabbed the extension.

"Hey," I said, expecting it to be Jamie or Caroline.

"Hey, Marit. I'm not disturbing you, am I?"

Noah. Just the sound of his voice made my heart speed up again. I paced around the room—nervous, excited.

"Not at all," I said, trying to make my voice sultry and seductive. "What's up?"

"I had a really good time last Friday," he said.

I shut my eyes for a second, sending a little prayer of thanks to the love gods.

"Didn't we cover this in Conversation yesterday?" I teased.

"Yeah, but we were speaking German," he countered. "I wanted to be sure you understood."

"I had a good time too," I told him.

"So . . . you want to do it again this weekend?" he asked.

Yes, yes, yes! I thought. *A thousand times yes!*

"Uh, sure," I said, trying to sound cool. "Do you have another lacrosse game?"

He chuckled, and I felt it all the way down to my toes. "No, but we could do the dinner part."

"That sounds great."

"Cool. So—Saturday night?"

I stopped short, remembering. "No, wait—I can't." My shoulders drooped with disappointment. "I have to go into the city with my family that night. My dad has a painting in a show."

There was a pause. Then Noah said, "I've never been to an art opening. . . ."

A warm feeling flooded through me. Noah was fishing for an invitation to my dad's show!

It was the perfect opportunity. Him, me, New York City— maybe we'd get to know each other better. Maybe we could move things along. . . .

But what about Jamie? He had assumed that he'd be coming with me. I couldn't just blow him off for a date with Noah. Could I?

No, I told myself. I wouldn't be blowing him off. I'd be making steps toward my ultimate goal—getting and keeping a boyfriend. A goal that Jamie knew about all along.

His feelings wouldn't be hurt, I reasoned. Especially if I found a way to soften the blow.

I decided then and there. This was an opportunity I simply could not pass up.

"Oh—do you want to come along?" I asked, mentally crossing my fingers.

"Absolutely," he told me. "It's a date."

"Yes, it is," I said.

Because this time? That's exactly how I was going to treat it. It was going to be me and Noah and the romantic fires kindling.

I just needed to figure out a way to break it to Jamie.

"I feel bad about leaving Caroline alone tomorrow night," I told Jamie, positive that a lightning bolt was about to strike me dead.

"I know." Jamie nodded. "But she wants to stay home to keep her mom company. What can we do?"

We'd been at the Tower Records in the mall after school for what felt like hours. Jamie had discovered a sale bin of seventies punk rock CDs and was tearing through it from top to bottom.

Every so often, he'd exclaim "Siouxie and the Banshees!" "Gang of Four!" "Generation X!" whenever he found a new group he liked.

I leaned against the jazz section and watched him, my stomach all in knots. It was Friday afternoon, and I hadn't found an easy way to un-invite him to the gallery show.

Time was running out.

"Caroline's mom is going to be at work practically the whole evening," I pointed out, not falsely. "Caroline will be sitting by herself all night. That can't be good for her."

Jamie didn't answer me—he had practically disappeared into the bin, trying to reach a Clash CD at the very bottom.

I took a deep breath. "So . . . I think one of us should stay with her."

Jamie struggled back upright and looked at me. "What?"

"One of us should be with her," I repeated. "I would stay, except my dad would be really upset if I didn't go to his opening." I paused. "Jamie, I just really think Caroline needs company tomorrow night."

I felt terrible about lying—or, rather, telling a half-truth—but I could feel that Noah and I were on the cusp of things. We had to have this date.

I'd figure out a way to make it up to Jamie later.

Jamie looked puzzled. "You don't want me to come to your dad's show?"

"Only because I'm worried about Caroline." I touched his arm, feeling so guilty I was sure my face was purple. "You understand, don't you?"

"I guess," Jamie said. "If you think that's what Caroline needs."

"I do," I told him. Then, desperate to change the subject, I pointed back into the bin. "Hey, is that a bootleg Black Flag album?"

"Where?" Jamie exclaimed, diving back in.

I leaned against the jazz records, just waiting for that lightning bolt.

Whenever my dad has a solo show or is getting a piece in a museum, the opening night parties are pretty low-key and fun—good music, lots of food, friendly people.

But when he has a piece in a group show, you never know what to expect. Sometimes it's unbelievably dull—wine and cheese and elevator music, with people shushing you nonstop.

On the opposite end of the spectrum are the openings where everybody gets drunk and the gallery owner acts like he's channeling Andy Warhol, trying to be as outrageous as possible.

I didn't know which it would be worse to bring Noah to—snoozeville or boozeville.

In truth, this opening surpassed them all. Because all the exhibits were abstract *nudes*! I had basically brought Noah to a peep show!

"Why didn't you warn me?" I hissed at my dad when Noah went to the men's room.

"What?" Dad asked innocently. "If you're going to be an artist, Marit, you can't be embarrassed by the human form."

I mumbled, "Fine," then hurried off to intercept Noah before my dad could launch into a lecture on the history of nudity in art or something.

I found Noah in front of my dad's painting, examining it closely. The picture looked, at first, like a bunch of green and gold blotches, but if you looked at it long enough, you could clearly see . . . *parts.*

I was terrified Noah would think it was a painting of my mom or something. But he turned to me and smiled.

"This is amazing. Your dad's brilliant."

"Thanks." There—that flutter in my heart again. Noah made it happen so easily. How could so much amazingness be wrapped up in just one guy?

We had walked around the gallery for an hour, looking at the paintings, when Noah stopped.

There was sound from my stomach like, *grrrrllgff.*

He gave me a crooked grin. "Did your stomach just growl?"

A combination of guilt and anticipation had kept me from eating anything since breakfast, and I was starving.

"What? No," I covered. I had barely gotten the sentence out when my stomach rumbled again.

"C'mon." Noah laughed. "Let's get you something to eat."

We walked over to the buffet and stared at it. For some reason, the catering had a Scandinavian theme. All the food was exotic, exquisite, and, to my way of thinking, completely inedible. Dishes of caviar, a giant carved-up fish with its head still attached, some odd greenish pâté covered in aspic.

Noah looked at me. "Would your dad be upset if we left for a while and grabbed some pizza?"

"Are you kidding? He'd probably want us to bring him back a piece," I answered.

We walked down the street to a place that served slices out of a tiny window in the side of a building. We carried our paper plates over to the stoop of a neighboring building and sat down to eat.

The night was warm, and we could hear music drifting out of someone's window, a woman singing along to a bluesy melody. The sidewalk was lined with trees, and little lights twinkled from the branches.

The pizza was delicious. Noah's shoulder was comfortably pressed up against mine. And I couldn't remember feeling happier.

"So—tell me about you," I said.

"Me?" Noah laughed. "What do you mean?"

"I mean, I know some things about you. Like, you moved here from Texas, you have a little brother, and you seem to be the physical embodiment of school spirit—"

He rolled his eyes, shoved my shoulder good-naturedly with his own.

"—but what about the rest? What did you do back in Texas?" I asked.

Noah let out a huge breath. "Well, back in Texas, I was on the lacrosse team."

"Naturally," I put in.

"I hung out with a good group of guys. Sammy, Joe, Brett—"

"Do you miss them?" I asked.

"I IM with them sometimes, but yeah," Noah admitted. "There were a lot of people I had to leave behind."

"Any girlfriends?" I asked.

"No one special," he admitted.

My heart gave a little thump.

"What about your mom?" I asked.

"My mom." He nodded slowly. "Honestly? I miss her most of all."

"Do you talk to her much now that you're here?"

He gazed out into the street, his eyes far away. "No. Not really. She's got . . ." He paused. "There are things she's dealing with."

"Tell me about them," I offered.

He shrugged. "There isn't much to tell. It's just, we can't really talk right now."

I placed a hand on his arm. "That must be hard."

He turned, smiled. "I think it's harder on Charlie. He loves my stepmom, but it's not the same, you know? I try to fill in the gaps. Keep him as occupied as I can so he won't think about it much."

I thought about all of Noah's commitments. The school play, lacrosse, the budding film club . . . I wondered if he was trying to keep himself occupied too.

I gave his arm a squeeze. "You're a good brother."

"Yeah?" He laughed. "Tell that to the Bionicle."

He was silent for a moment; then he continued. "I could let it get to me, being away from home, my friends. But you know, I've found a lot to like here too."

"Really?" I asked.

Noah stared at me a moment. "Yeah," he whispered.

Notes drifted down from the apartment above us, smooth and low. A light breeze rustled the leaves in the trees.

"I have to tell you," he said, his gaze returning to a point across the street. "After the bonfire? I thought you'd never speak to me again."

I felt myself blushing. "Oh my God. I'm still so sorry about that."

"You don't need to be," Noah said. "I just don't know why you ran away. I mean, did I do something wrong?"

"Oh God, no," I told him. "It was me. All me. I was just . . . scared."

Noah scoffed. "I find that hard to believe. Any girl who isn't afraid of Juliet Hammond can't be scared of much."

I laughed. "Thanks, but it's the truth."

His eyes searched mine. "What were you scared of?"

I paused. That was the question, wasn't it?

"I guess, when it comes down to it, it was the uncertainty," I said. "The being unsure of myself and what I was doing. It just made it . . . hard to deal."

"Well, let me tell you what I'm certain of," Noah said. "I am certain that you are the most interesting person that I have ever met. You are different, Marit. One of a kind."

"You say that like it's a good thing," I joked.

"It is," he said. "You don't follow the crowd. You're just— who you are."

He gestured to my paper plate. "You done with that?"

I finished my slice, and Noah carried our plates over to a trash can and threw them away.

Then he held out his hands and pulled me to my feet. But instead of letting go, he twirled me around. Then he pulled me closer.

He put his arms around me and gazed down into my eyes.

This, I thought, my pulse racing. *This is what I have been missing. This fizzy dizziness that is not fear and not lust but something wholly, entirely different.*

"How are you feeling now?" he asked, the twinkling city lights dancing in his eyes. "Afraid?"

I answered honestly. "No."

Noah ducked his head and brushed his lips against mine.

I tilted my face up and brought my mouth to his.

I poured everything I was feeling into that kiss. And standing there, in his arms, I could feel great, huge things happening—my life changing—the earth spinning around on its axis.

I wasn't focused on lips or mouths or anything physical. The only thing in my mind was *Noah.*

I lost all sense of time as we stood there on the busy sidewalk. I kissed him until my lips were sore and my knees were ready to buckle.

We broke apart. I smiled up at him. All I could think at that moment was that there was so much to him. So much more than anybody knew.

The way he'd reacted to my dad's painting, the way he didn't care about my disdain for school activities, even the way he made those activities seem not so bad after all . . .

He wasn't just a one-man pep squad. He was different than any other boy I'd ever been with.

Pop!

Eric and all the other guys had just been puppy-love crushes. And though I adored Jamie with my whole heart, there was always something missing with him, some disconnect between friendship and romance that we could never bridge.

Noah was everything I'd been looking for. His arms around me felt *right*, in a way I had never experienced before.

He tilted back his head and looked into my eyes. "You look so far away," he said. "What are you thinking?"

I simply smiled, but inside I was thinking, *This is true. This is right. It may sound crazy, but somehow, I belong with Noah.*

And some way, I have to break it to Jamie.

20

When Jamie got to my house the next Saturday, I had a speech all rehearsed and all ready to go. But before I had a chance to say a word, he pulled me to him and started kissing me.

God. How could something that felt so right just a week ago seem so wrong?

I couldn't prevent a quick fantasy flashing through my mind—*Noah* kissing me, *Noah* reaching for me—

I flashed back to reality, and the reason I needed to come clean was perfectly clear.

"Hey," I said, taking a step back, "are you hungry? Want to get a snack?"

Jamie was quiet for a second.

"Jamie?"

He grinned. "Sorry—there are just so many dirty responses to that, I was trying to figure out which one to go with."

I rolled my eyes and swatted his arm. "Let's get something to eat."

He followed me to the kitchen, and I started pulling stuff out of the fridge.

"I could make grilled cheese," I told him, "except we don't have any bread. So, your choice: I can make it on a tortilla or a hot dog bun."

"I don't want anything to eat," Jamie said. He took my hand and gently tugged me back over to him so he could kiss me some more.

But I was untuggable. "Jamie. Listen, I was just—I've been thinking. About us. About our—arrangement."

Jamie didn't answer, but he *did* stop trying to kiss me. So I plunged ahead.

"I'm not sure that it's such a good idea that we keep doing what we've been doing."

"Is something wrong?" he asked, concerned. "Are you okay?"

"I'm fine, everything's fine," I said, "It's just—"

I put a hand on his chest, resting over his heart.

"Jamie. The whole point of us having had sex in the first place was so I could find a boyfriend, right?"

"Right—" he said uncertainly.

God, this was hard. How could I say it without hurting his feelings?

"You remember our pact? How we said we'd stay friends and not let the sex change our friendship or get in the way at all?"

He nodded, his expression unreadable.

"Here's the thing—I want a boyfriend."

There. I said it. I ripped off the Band-Aid.

Jamie blinked. "You want—a boyfriend?"

I hurried to explain. "Jamie, you have to know I would die before I would risk hurting our friendship. But since the first day of school, my goal has been to fall in love and have a boyfriend and go to prom and all of that. So . . ."

"So now our whole arrangement doesn't make sense," Jamie said, his voice calm and completely normal.

I nodded and silently rejoiced. He understood! He didn't even seem to be angry about it.

Jamie really was the coolest guy I knew. And someday he was going to make some girl very happy.

Before I could say anything more, Jamie's cell phone rang.

He glanced at it. "My mom," he told me, opening the phone.

"Hey, Mom." He paused. "Yeah, I can be there in a few minutes. Okay, I'm on my way."

He snapped his phone shut.

"Computer trouble," he explained. "If I don't get over there soon, the hard drive is toast. I'm sorry—but can we talk about this later?"

"Sure," I said, mildly relieved.

I could definitely tell him about Noah later. I'd already gotten the hard part out of the way, and maybe it was better to break the news to Jamie one piece at a time.

"So, are we . . . ?" I trailed off, not sure of the question I wanted to ask.

Jamie gave me a crooked smile. "Yes."

Then he leaned forward and kissed me one last time. It was a soft, gentle kiss. A goodbye kiss.

Gratitude flooded my heart.

It was the sweetest way to end things.

Jamie started toward his car. I shut the door behind him, thanking my lucky stars that I had such great friends.

21

When my family got home that night, they were in better moods than I'd seen them in for months. My mom was actually singing as she carried her overnight bag upstairs, and my dad dropped a kiss on the top of my head before heading up after her.

Hilly came trailing in after them, and I almost didn't recognize the smiling girl standing in front of me as my sister.

"Trip went well?" I asked, looking up from the table where I was doing homework.

"Bryn Mawr is amazing!" Hilly said. "And they have January admissions, so if they accepted me, I could start after Christmas! I'd only be a semester behind!"

Wow. "That must have made Tom and Elena happy," I said.

Pop!

"You have no idea." She sank down in a chair across from me and shut her eyes, a happy smile on her face.

I was about to go back to my calculus problem when all of a sudden her eyes snapped open and she straightened up in her chair.

"Oh my God, I can't believe I almost forgot—how did things go with Jamie?!"

"Good. Really good," I told her, unable to stop myself from grinning.

"He took it well?"

"Better than I would have thought possible."

Hilly smiled. "Looks like we both got what we wished for."

She knocked twice on the table for luck. Then she got up and headed upstairs.

22

Right after school on Friday, Noah and I headed out to take his brother, Charlie, to a Halloween haunted house sponsored by the local Cub Scout troop.

Noah met me at my locker, and we headed out toward the student parking lot, telling each other our favorite things we'd ever been for Halloween.

"When I was eight, I dressed up as the girl who gets shot out of the cannon at the circus," I confessed.

"That is so weird," Noah said, laughing.

"No, it's not! It was cool," I said. "My mom sewed sequins onto this red, white, and blue bathing suit I had, and I wore a helmet, go-go boots, and a cape with the edges singed, and I carried a basketball I'd painted black like a cannonball."

Noah shook his head. "Twisted."

As we walked, Noah caught my hand in his. He laced his fingers through mine, swinging our arms between us.

I secretly bit my lip. It felt like my whole body was smiling.

The last few days at school had been amazing. Noah and I barely ran into each other, but somehow he still found ways to be romantic.

In German Conversation he asked, *"Was ist deine Lieblingsblume?"*

The next morning I found a sprig of orchids stuck in one of the slats of my locker.

Luckily, I had gotten to school early that day, so Jamie hadn't seen the flowers.

I still hadn't found the right opportunity to tell Jamie about Noah—and I'd tried, really, I had. But Caroline was at my house all the time now, so it was difficult to get a second alone.

It didn't matter, I told myself. I was sure the moment would present itself soon.

"Whatever happened to dressing up like a princess or a ballerina?" Noah teased as we made our way to his car.

"And look like every other girl on the block? No way," I told him.

Noah squeezed my hand. "I bet you looked cute in go-go boots."

I smirked. "Maybe I'll dress up again this Halloween, and you can see for yourself."

We reached his car, and he let go of my hand while he dug around in his pocket for his keys.

I looked at my watch. "You know, we've got a ton of time before the haunted house opens."

Noah glanced at his own watch. "You're right. We've got two hours to kill."

"So what should we do while we're waiting?" I asked. Noah took my hand and pulled me close. He bent his head like he was going to kiss me. But then he stopped with his lips a fraction of an inch from mine. "I don't know. You got any ideas?"

"We could . . . practice solving binomial theorems," I teased. "Although Charlie wouldn't be interested in that."

"Probably not," he agreed. "Any other ideas?"

"Skeet shooting?" I offered.

He shook his head. "Not a good activity for a five-year-old."

"Bird-watching?"

His lips were still inches from mine, and the tension was about to make me insane.

"Uh-uh."

"Then I'm out of ideas," I told him. "Can't you think up *something* for us to do?"

"I know," he said. "How about this?"

I shut my eyes, waiting to be kissed.

But instead of kissing me, he blew a raspberry on my cheek! I shrieked and squirmed away from him.

"What? You don't like my suggestion?"

"No!" I said, my eyes wide, laughing.

Emberly and a couple of the other minor Pradas sneered at us from across the lot.

Let them, I thought. *Who cares what they think?*

Noah grabbed me by the shoulders and blew a raspberry on my other cheek.

I shrieked again. "Noah! Stop that!"

"What if I do *this*?" He leaned forward again and this time kissed me for real, absolutely taking my breath away.

I closed my eyes, lost in the sensation.

Until someone called my name.

"Marit?"

I opened my eyes and saw Jamie staring at me, a shocked expression on his face.

Oh no.

This was not the way I wanted Jamie to find out about Noah and me.

Caroline came walking up behind him and froze when she saw us.

"Hi," I said weakly. "I thought the two of you were . . . studying in the library."

Jamie's eyes bored into mine. "We changed our minds."

"Hey, guys. How's it going?" Noah asked, completely oblivious.

Jamie ticked his gaze away from me. "What are you doing?" he asked Noah, his voice sounding strangled.

"We're going to a haunted house," Noah told him. "Do you guys want to—"

"No," Jamie cut him off. "I mean, what are you doing *kissing my girlfriend?*"

What? I blinked at Jamie, confused. *His girlfriend?* What was he talking about?

Noah looked from me to Jamie, a half smile on his face, like he was waiting to get the joke. "*Your* girlfriend?"

Jamie nodded angrily. "Yes, *my girlfriend*. You want to get your hands off her?"

"Jamie," I said, genuinely confused, "what are you talking about?"

"I'm talking about this Neanderthal jock trying to kiss you when you and I are supposed to be a couple!"

I blinked and swallowed hard.

Something had gone terribly wrong, but I wasn't sure when or how it happened.

I shot a glance over at Emberly and her friends. Their antennae were way up. I wouldn't be surprised if they were actually taking notes.

Noah gave me a puzzled look, then put up his hands to placate Jamie. "Dude, I know you guys are friends and all, but Marit and I are dating."

Jamie stared at him, incredulous. *"Dude,"* he said bitterly. "She's in love with me!"

Everyone was quiet. They all turned to face me.

"Jamie, that's not true," I said softly.

All the blood drained from Jamie's face. "But—but you said—"

"I'm with Noah. We're dating." I tried to speak gently. "I'm sorry I didn't—"

He interrupted then, his voice barely a whisper. "When?"

"I've always liked him," I admitted, feeling myself blush at the words.

Noah put a warm hand against my back. "Me too," he told Jamie. "And ever since the gallery opening that Saturday night—"

"Saturday night?" Jamie exclaimed, and my heart plummeted to my knees.

"Yeah, Saturday. We went to her dad's art opening," Noah said, oblivious to the fact that with that one sentence, he was ruining my life.

Caroline let out a little squeak. She finally moved, putting her hand on Jamie's sleeve and ineffectually tugging at it.

Blood returned to Jamie's face, two bright blotches of red on his cheeks. His expression hardened. He worked his jaw, his voice turning mean.

"Okay," he said to Noah. "Okay, maybe you went to her

dad's thing on Saturday. But tell me this, how is Marit *your* girlfriend *when she's sleeping with me?*"

Oh my God. The world tilted beneath me.

Jamie stared hard. "Tell him, Marit."

Caroline yanked at Jamie's shirt, but he didn't budge.

"Tell him!" he yelled at me.

Everything went black for a moment, and my ears were filled with a harsh buzzing noise. I felt like I was going to faint or throw up or burst into flames.

Finally Caroline managed to pull Jamie away, and, too late, they disappeared around the side of the school.

Noah's mouth was hanging open. "Marit? What the hell was that?"

But I couldn't look at him, couldn't bear to see the way he was surely looking at me.

I mumbled, "I'm sorry," and fled, chasing Jamie and Caroline out of sight.

23

I caught up with them by the athletic fields where the lacrosse team holds its practices.

"What the hell was that?" I demanded, rage making all the hairs on my head bristle.

Jamie kept going, pushing past me. I moved to follow him, but Caroline whirled around, blocking my way.

"I told you this was going to happen!" she said. "I warned you to be careful."

"I was careful!" I exclaimed. "I broke up with him! I have no idea how he could have thought I was in love with him."

She stared at me, a look of disbelief on her face. "He thought that because *he* was in love with *you!*"

I blinked. Was I hearing her right?

"What are you talking about?"

"Marit," Caroline started, "he's in love with you. He's *always* been in love with you, but you are too clueless and—and *selfish* to see it!"

My mind whirled. It couldn't be true, could it? Jamie didn't feel that way about me, did he?

"It's not possible," I told her. "He—he never said anything. He never even gave me a sign."

"Please." Caroline let out a snort. "All he gave you were signs." She started ticking them off on her fingers. "Checking up on you after the bonfire. Agreeing to sleep with you after he saw Noah put his arm around you. The way he's hated every boyfriend you've ever had. The mix tape he made you. Asking you to *dance* to the mix tape—"

"Wait a minute," I interrupted. "How do you know about all these things?"

"Because *I'm* the one he comes crying to when you step all over his heart! Think about it, Marit. You were the first girl that Jamie's been with—for anything. You were his first *kiss*. His first *date*."

"Then why didn't you ever say anything?"

"I tried to tell you!" Caroline insisted. "You just didn't listen."

No, I thought. No, this wasn't right.

"*He's* the one who didn't listen," I said. "I *told* him I wanted a boyfriend, so the sleeping-together-as-just-friends thing wasn't working out. How in the world did he get the idea that we were a couple?"

"You tell me," Caroline spat.

I replayed the scene in my mind. Jamie's words, the gentle kiss.

Wait—oh my God.

When I said I wanted a boyfriend . . . did Jamie think I meant *him*?

"I can't believe this is happening," I said softly.

"I warned you to be careful of his feelings," Caroline said.

And with that, she pushed past me and walked away.

I don't know how long I stood there, replaying the conversation in my mind. But when I headed back toward the parking lot, Noah was waiting for me, leaning against his car with his arms folded across his chest.

The Pradas had gone, I noted, no doubt hard at work already, spreading news about our little scene.

Better to get this over with, I decided. I walked up to Noah.

"Listen—" I started to say, but he held up one finger to stop me.

"First? We've got some unfinished business to take care of."

He leaned forward and kissed me. Just a small, sweet peck on the lips.

I stood there, too dumbfounded to speak.

"Good," he said when he'd pulled away. "No interruptions. Now, you still want to go to the haunted house?"

I nodded, mute.

We got in the car and Noah pulled out onto the street. He was acting completely normal, but I was freaking out. Why was he being so chill about this?

"Listen," I said to him, "about before—I'm really sorry about what Jamie—"

Noah smiled and shrugged. "It's cool. Can't blame the guy for being jealous."

"Um . . . you can't?"

Noah grinned and gave my shoulder a playful shove. "He wants you for himself, so he made up that stuff to try to scare me off."

I paused for a second, trying to figure it all out.

Noah thought Jamie was lying. It was, in one way, a lucky turn of events. But wasn't it wrong to let him keep believing it?

Yes. I knew it was. And somehow I had to find a way to tell Noah the truth. . . .

But not now. Everything was too new. There was no way he would understand.

"Marit?" Noah's voice broke through my thoughts. I could see doubt creeping onto his face. "He *was* making it up, right?"

I would tell Noah the truth, I decided. Just—later.

"Yeah," I told him. "I can't believe he pretended we'd been anything more than just friends."

"You *don't* have feelings for him, do you?" Noah asked quietly.

This time I was able to answer truthfully. "No. Not the kind you mean."

I thought for a minute, then added, "But I do really love him as a friend, and I feel terrible about hurting him."

"Hey, it's not your fault," Noah said. "You can't help being so smokin' that every guy you meet falls for you."

I gave a rueful laugh, and he turned serious again.

"Do you want to go talk to him now? I'll drive you there. We can take a rain check on tonight."

I gazed at Noah's profile, outlined against the car window, and wondered—was there ever a more thoughtful person?

"No, I think a haunted house would be way less scary than dealing with Jamie and Caroline right now. Besides, they're upset. I think I should wait until they calm down a little."

"Okay." Noah nodded.

I hunched down in my seat, bitter. "Right at this moment? They're probably talking about what an ogre I am."

"Hey, they'll come around. Just give it time. And until they do"—Noah smiled and gave a little shrug—"you've got me."

"Thanks," I told him. I moved closer on the wide front seat and rested my head against his warm, strong shoulder.

A tear escaped from the corner of my eye.

There was a time when I thought that having Noah would be the answer to my problems.

But now, my best friends in the world weren't speaking to me.

My problems, it seemed, were just beginning.

24

I woke up the next morning, my head still swimming about the whole Jamie fiasco.

I still couldn't believe what Caroline had said.

And I *really* couldn't believe that I hadn't seen the truth myself.

How could I have missed the fact that Jamie was in love with me?

I replayed all of our conversations in my mind. Everything that had happened since the start of school.

Jamie ragging on my ex-boyfriends. Jamie saying I was the hottest girl at Sterling. Jamie's knee-jerk reaction to Noah. And his expression when we were together that last time.

Were there signs? Yes.

Had I purposely ignored them?

I didn't think so.

I had to talk to him, I decided. I had to make Jamie see that I had just been—clueless.

And if I had known the truth—if *he had told it to me*—I would have handled things very, very differently.

But first I needed to get Caroline back on my side, to help me persuade Jamie to listen.

I dialed her number and—

"Hi, it's Caroline. Leave a message." *Beep!*

Oh my God, was she *screening* me? There's no way she'd have left the house this early.

"Um, hey, it's me. Call me, okay?"

I hung up, trying to decide what to do next.

Well, it couldn't hurt to talk to Jamie first. . . .

His mom answered, then shouted up the stairs for Jamie to pick up. After a minute she came back to the phone.

"I'm sorry, he's not answering, Marit. Maybe he's still sleeping."

Jamie was a morning person, so I knew for sure that wasn't true.

"Oh," I said. "Can you just have him call me when he wakes up?"

"Sure," his mom told me.

I hung up, dejected.

They weren't going to call me back. Not today.

But we'd been friends for so long—they had to give me a chance to try to make things right. Didn't they?

I moped around all weekend, with no word from either Jamie or Caroline.

Monday and Tuesday were no better. I was being ignored by my friends and—thanks to the Pradas—gossiped about by everyone else. I could handle the rumors, but the silent treatment? That was tough.

And lunch was the worst. When I got to the cafeteria, I saw Caroline glaring at me from our usual table. My heart sank as I realized that I should probably sit elsewhere until things got straightened out.

I looked around for an empty seat and found Dana waving at me. Her table was smack in front of the vice principal's office, possibly the worst place in the entire cafeteria, but I was thrilled just to have a place to put my tray down.

"Hey, Dana," I said as I slipped into a chair on Tuesday, the second day of my exile.

"Hey." Dana smiled sympathetically. "How's the Sterling rumor mill treating you?"

"About as well as it treated you," I told her. I shoved half a fish stick in my mouth, trying not to gag.

"Yeah." Dana nodded. "It sucks. But you know, I was thinking about what you told me yesterday, and this whole deal with you and Jamie? I don't think it's that big a thing.

Half the school already thought you and Jamie were hooking up anyway, you hang out with him so much."

"I guess," I said. "But Jamie was already mad. People talking about it is only making it worse."

Dana shook her head. "Everyone either thinks he's a stooge because he was played or a loser because he made the whole thing up."

I sighed. "Why can't people just mind their own business?"

Dana laughed. "Mind their own business! At this school?" Her eyes ticked over to the Pradas' table. "Rick Fielding and his crew pretty much ruined my life. When I told him I wouldn't sleep with him, he decided to tell the whole school that I slept with anyone who was willing. And *everyone* believed him."

Now it was my turn to look sympathetic. "Well, at least you know you didn't do anything *wrong*."

Dana chuckled. "Marit. I'm seventeen and I'm pregnant. Clearly, I did *something* wrong."

I gave a dry laugh and toyed with my side salad. "I don't care about the rumors. I care about getting my friends back."

"Hey, don't worry," she told me. "It's never too late. A misunderstanding like yours can be fixed."

I frowned and nibbled on a piece of lettuce.

"Marit. Really. It's not like this has to have *permanent* consequences." Her hand subconsciously went back to her belly.

"So what am I supposed to do?" I asked her. "They won't listen to me! Whenever I try to approach them, they close ranks. Jamie has even cut orchestra for the past two days!"

"*Make* them listen," she encouraged.

She slid a newspaper across the table. I looked down at it. An ad in the lower left-hand corner was circled in red.

"They'll come around," Dana encouraged. "You'll see."

I stared at the ad, and for a moment I felt a little bit of hope. I looked up at Dana, and for once she actually *was* glowing.

Huh, I thought. Hope, delivered courtesy of your friendly neighborhood teenage mom.

I got to the theater early and bought a ticket. Then I sat down on one of the musty velvet benches in the lobby.

I was praying that Jamie had seen the ad for the Fellini retrospective because if he had, I knew he'd show.

I *also* knew there was no way on earth he'd be able to drag Caroline along with him.

Strategy of the day? Divide and conquer.

A couple of artsy-hippie people drifted past, going into the theater, and then Jamie appeared, clutching a ticket, by himself.

He froze when he spotted me. I jumped up from the bench, ready to chase him down the street if I had to, but instead he walked over to me and stood there, waiting.

"I'm sorry," I said. "I'm so sorry."

"Okay," he said, and started to leave.

I reached out a hand to stop him. "Jamie, wait. Can't we talk about this?"

He turned back. "Talk."

I had no idea what to say to him. "Jamie, I mean, this is *crazy*. Caroline says you're in love with me—"

Jamie looked away, but I pushed on.

"How come you never told me? How could you sleep with me without telling me?"

"Because I thought—" He let out a shaky breath. "I thought maybe that if we slept together, you'd fall in love with me too."

"But why didn't you just *tell* me?" I repeated. "Why weren't you just honest about how you felt—"

Jamie's voice took on a hard edge. "Oh, like you were honest?"

"Jamie—"

"You lied to me. You lied about Noah."

"I told you I wanted a boyfriend," I said. "I didn't realize you misunderstood."

"So how come you didn't tell me you were going out with him?" he asked. "If you didn't feel guilty about seeing him, why did you keep it a secret?"

"I didn't want to hurt you," I said quietly. "And it never seemed like the right time—"

Jamie snorted, but I continued. "We had a pact—a pact *that I believed in.* You promised me we would stay friends no matter what."

"Well, too late for that," he said flatly.

I took a deep breath, trying to hold it together.

"Jamie. We've been friends for eight years. We've only been more than that for three *weeks.* We've got to find a way to work through this."

Jamie didn't say anything.

"Please," I continued. "I can't stand fighting with you. I can't stand the fact that I hurt you. If I had known how you were feeling, I would have handled everything differently because I'm so sorry and I miss you so much and I can't go on like this."

Jamie shut his eyes for a minute. When he opened them again, his face was blank and impassive. "What do you want me to say, Marit? That I'm not mad? That you didn't hurt me?" He shrugged. "I can't say any of that. Sorry."

He turned and walked into the movie theater.

I looked at the ticket in my hand, then tossed it in the trash and headed home.

25

I tried to tell myself that I was looking forward to my date with Noah on Saturday night.

"Wow, a whole evening with someone who isn't mad at me!" I cheered, a bit too enthusiastically.

But as soon as we were alone together, I couldn't help talking about the only thing that occupied my mind—my so-called, probably ex-best friends.

"So they're still mad, huh?" Noah asked.

He glanced over at me, then returned his eyes to the road, pointing the car toward the Greenwich Multiplex.

"Yeah." I sighed. "It's like they hate me. At this point, I'm just waiting for graduation so at least it'll be less obvious that they aren't talking to me."

"Hey, come on now," Noah said, "it's not that bad. Besides, you didn't do anything wrong."

I flushed guiltily, remembering my many half-truths. Including the one I was currently allowing Noah to believe. "Yeah . . ."

"Honestly? I just think it's going to take a little time."

"It's been more than a week already," I complained. "How much time do they need?"

Noah gave me a crooked smile. "I don't know them that well, but it seems like Caroline practically lives at your house. I bet in a couple of days, she'll have forgotten about the whole thing."

"Wouldn't count on it," I muttered. "And what about Jamie?"

Noah twisted his mouth around, considering. "That might take a little longer," he admitted. "But I bet once he starts dating someone else, he'll get over it completely."

"That could take forever!" I wailed. "Jamie's never dated anyone in his life."

"Well, I don't know. Maybe he can, like, build a girl robot or something."

I giggled, feeling a twinge of guilt as I did. "Wait—a *girl robot*? How big a geek do you think Jamie is?"

Noah started laughing too. "I know he's your bud and all,

but you've got to admit, that kid is about as geeky as they come."

"He is not!" I said, suddenly offended on Jamie's behalf. "He's just . . . artistic."

"Right. Artistic. He's probably making up new Dungeons and Dragons characters as we speak."

Now he'd gone too far.

"Don't go knocking D&D," I warned him.

Noah's eyes widened. "Tell me you're joking. You don't actually play, do you?"

"My dad was a Dungeon Master when he was in college, and when I was in elementary school, our whole family used to play D&D together every weekend."

"Hmph. That's actually pretty cool," Noah said. "My family never played anything more adventurous than Uno."

"Well, we played our fair share of that too."

Noah pulled into a parking spot at the movie theater. But he didn't turn the car off. Instead he sat there, staring at me, a little smirk flitting across his mouth.

"What?" I finally demanded.

He glanced at me out of the corner of his eye. "So, what was your character, some sort of evil pixie?"

"As if," I told him. "I was an eighth-level fighter elf named Fausto."

"Sexy," he joked. He parked the car and shut off the engine. "Will you show me some of your fighter moves later?"

I shook my head. "I've had enough fighting this week."

Noah slung an arm around my shoulders and we headed into the theater.

"So what are we seeing?" I asked.

"German film," Noah said. "A postwar portrayal of disillusionment. The story of the saddest clown ever to put on face paint."

I stared at him. Seconds ticked by.

Finally he cracked a smile.

"Bruckheimer film. Lots of explosions and alien ass-kicking."

I smiled. "Sounds like heaven."

Noah grabbed my hand. "Come on. I'll buy you some popcorn."

Monday morning Dana had an appointment with her obstetrician, so I was lunching solo. I was sitting at her table, minding my own business, when—

"Marit!" Juliet Hammond called. She waved at me, her evil posse in tow. "Can we sit with you?"

"Yeah." I pretended to crack up, then returned to my baked macaroni. "Good one."

"I'm *serious*," she said, rolling her eyes.

Then, without an invitation, she and her coven descended, filling the little table right in front of the vice principal's office.

"What the hell are you doing?" I yelped as Juliet squeezed in next to me.

"Well, now that you and Noah are dating, we're probably

going to be seeing a lot of each other," Juliet explained. "Isn't it time we buried the hatchet?"

I hesitated. She had a point. I'd formed my opinion about these kids in elementary school. Maybe if I got to know them better, I'd see what sweet, kind, lovely people they actually were.

Right. And maybe the Louvre would take down the *Mona Lisa* and hang up one of my paintings instead.

I was painfully aware of Jamie's and Caroline's eyes on me. Studying my every move.

God, I thought, could things get any worse?

"Do you know everybody?" Juliet said, waving her hand around the table by way of introduction. "Everybody, this is Marit. She's dating Noah."

Most of the kids at the table nodded or waved, and a couple of girls said "hi."

I gave them a little wave, feeling slightly ill.

"So, Marit. Did you buy your homecoming dress yet?" Emberly asked me. "I got mine at Dolce weeks ago. It's so pretty; it's like this shimmery blue—"

She broke off in the middle of her description as Caroline and Jamie got up from their table and stormed past us on their way out of the cafeteria.

"Unbelievable," Caroline muttered as she walked by my chair. "You are such a traitor."

"Hey—" I started to protest, but then Jamie was standing in front of me.

Juliet's friends became aware of the drama. They all stopped talking and looked up at Jamie expectantly.

Jamie didn't say anything. He stared at me for a long minute, his jaw working. Then he turned and fled, banging into Rick Fielding, who was on his way to the table.

"What's up, freak boy?" Rick mocked him.

Jamie stuttered something, then ran past him and out of the cafeteria.

All of Juliet's friends burst out laughing.

"What a *loser*," said one of them, an emaciated cheerleader sitting across from me.

"He's not a loser," I told them, watching him go. "He's a good friend."

"Some friend," Juliet scoffed, "spreading those rumors about you."

"Oh my God, I can't believe all that stuff he said," Emberly sympathized. "That's *so* wrong."

"Jamie didn't start those rumors," I told them, starting to get mad. "Somebody else did. Someone I think you know *very well*."

Rick squeezed in next to Juliet. "What difference does it make?" he asked. "Either way, the kid's delusional. Like anyone would pick him over Noah."

"Like anyone would pick him at all," the skinny cheer-leader said.

Everyone laughed again.

"Ooh, I heard he had a crush on this majorette from Stamford, and she had to get a restraining order against him 'cause he was stalking her," Emberly said.

"What?! That's not true," I told them.

"I heard he saw Lindsay Lohan on the street in Manhattan once, and he told everybody they hooked up," Juliet joined in.

"I heard he paid that skank Dana fifty bucks to let him touch her boob." The skinny cheerleader laughed.

"He did not!" I shouted. "You're making up all these lies about him. None of that never happened."

"Ooh, sounds like someone is defending her boyfriend." It was Ms. Emaciated again.

The other kids laughed, and Juliet raised an eyebrow.

"Really, Marit, why are you getting so mad?" She affected a pouty little frown. "Is it that Jamie really is your boyfriend? Does the truth hurt?"

I stood and gathered my stuff.

"You guys are a bunch of assholes," I told them. "You know perfectly well Jamie didn't do any of those things. You're making it up just to feel superior. But really? All you are is pathetic."

They smirked at me.

"You *love* him!" Juliet said, her eyes wide.

"I do not!"

Rick leaned back in his chair and scratched his stomach. "Wow, if you had sex with that little geek, you must be even skankier than Dana."

I snapped. "Hey, Dana's a friend of mine, jerk. Stop spreading rumors about her, and don't you dare start spreading them about Jamie."

Rick scowled at me. "I would, except that *Jamie* was the one who told everyone you slept with him. We didn't start that—he did. So I guess that means it's true."

Juliet squealed and clapped. "Oh my God, it's true! You had sex with Jamie!"

"Yes, I did!" I shouted, frustrated. "I had sex with Jamie Lyons. So what?"

"So that makes him—and you—even bigger losers than I thought," Rick scoffed.

"That *makes it* none of your business," I yelled. "You disgusting, backstabbing . . . assface!"

I shoved back my chair and grabbed my tray. Then I turned and stomped out of the cafeteria.

I don't know how I made it through gym class, my stomach was churning so badly. When the bell rang at the end of the period, I skipped my shower and raced down the hall to German, desperate to find Noah.

If I knew anything about Sterling, it was that word circulated quickly—especially where the Pradas were concerned. I needed to get to Noah to explain my cafeteria explosion—before he heard it from someone else.

He was in his seat when I walked in. He barely looked up as I sat down next to him. My heart twisted as I realized what had happened.

"You heard?" I asked, lightly touching his arm.

He gazed at me unemotionally. "Yes."

"I'm sorry. I wanted to tell you myself." The words tumbled out of my mouth. "They were making fun of Jamie. I *had* to defend him. Even though he's mad at me right now, he's my friend."

"Sounds to me like he's more than just a friend," he answered, his voice level.

"Noah, he's not," I reassured him.

Noah regarded me carefully, his eyes filled with doubt.

"So you haven't ever had sex with him?" he asked. "And if you could respect me enough to tell me the truth this time . . ."

I panicked. I had no idea how to explain what Jamie and I really were. Not without ruining everything Noah and I had together. I felt like bursting into tears, but instead I just said, "It's complicated."

Noah didn't say anything for a minute; then he sighed.

"Let's just do our conversation." He looked down at his book. *"Wie heisst der Roman den du mir empfohlen hast?"*

"Noah, please—" I said in a voice that was barely a whisper. "It didn't mean anything. I like *you*."

"Then why did you lie to me?"

"I thought—I was afraid you wouldn't like me if you knew," I said softly. "I'm sorry."

"Listen," Noah said, leaning back in his seat, away from me, "you're a cool girl and all, but I think for now we should probably just be—"

"Friends?" I asked, but he shook his head.

"Conversation partners."

My face started to burn. I was afraid for Noah to see my reaction, but he was already looking down at his textbook.

"Wer hat dir das Buch gegeben?"

I lowered my eyes to my own book to try and find an answer. But the words swam as tears filled my eyes.

"Wer hat dir das Buch gegeben?" Noah repeated.

I closed my book and ran from the room.

For the first time ever in my life, I ditched school and walked home. Whatever punishment they could give me would be nothing compared to the torture of having to finish the day.

I let myself into the kitchen and sat down at the dining

table. I thought about crying, but I was just too exhausted. Besides, it wasn't like crying would get Noah to like me again or my friends to speak to me.

I was still sitting there in my coat, staring off at nothing a half an hour later, when the back door opened and my father came in. He gave a start when he saw me and came rushing over.

"Marit? What are you doing home? Are you okay? Did something happen?"

"I'm okay," I said in a tiny voice. "I just . . . couldn't be at school anymore."

Dad looked at me for a long moment, with something like understanding on his face. "Tell you what, how about you come down to the studio with me and do some painting? We'll count that as your schoolwork for today. I'll write you a note so you won't get in trouble for cutting class."

That was the best offer I'd had in what felt like forever, so I got up from my chair and followed him to the studio.

"I think we should try the inner portrait exercise again," Dad said, setting a fresh canvas on my easel.

Oh God. If I had to face my inner self right now, it would absolutely, positively, one hundred percent kill me.

"I'm really not feeling it today," I said. "Can we maybe just do a still life or something? Bowl of fruit and jug of wine? Or what about that last one I did—*Can of Soda*. You loved it, remember?"

But he shook his head. "The days you aren't 'feeling it' are the days when it is most important to do it anyway."

"Is this painting or therapy?" I groused, going to select my colors.

"Both!" he shouted. "You think when van Gogh cut off his ear, he took the day off to moan and groan?"

"Probably."

"Wrong. That was the exact same day he began painting *The Starry Night*. He turned his inner turmoil into his greatest masterpiece."

I frowned. "Really?"

Dad shrugged and gave me a crooked grin. "I have no idea. But wouldn't it be cool if it was true?"

He dropped a kiss on the top of my head, then pointed me to my easel.

I squeezed the different-colored oils onto my palette as Dad crossed to the CD player and slid in a disc.

Despite my bad mood, I had to laugh when I heard the opening bars of the first song. "The *Evita* sound track?"

"Another example of turning tragedy into greatness. Now get to work!"

I started painting, but right away I could tell my rhythm was off.

The colors looked different on the canvas than they did in the tube, my brush went in directions I wasn't expecting, and the picture just didn't take on the shape I wanted it to.

I glanced over at my dad, but he was completely absorbed in his own painting.

I added more and more layers of paint, but each thing I tried only made it worse.

I was getting frustrated, and it was showing in the piece. The last time I'd tried this exercise, the resulting portrait may have been a bit of a jumble, but at least it evoked a specific mood or emotion.

This time? There was no cohesion, no unity, just a big muddy splotch. Finally I threw down my brush, and my dad looked over the top of his own canvas at me.

"Keep going," he called.

"But this isn't working," I told him. "All I've done is waste paint and make a big mess."

"*Life* is messy. Your assignment was to paint your inner portrait. If your emotions are in turmoil, that's going to show on your canvas." He put his brush down and walked over to me. "That makes your painting a success, not a mess."

He stopped in front of my canvas and leaned close to examine it. He stared at the painting, then put his arm around my shoulders and gave me a squeeze.

"Oh, honey," he said. "Whatever it is, it'll be all right."

27

The next morning I woke up with a new determination. As sad as I was about Noah, I'd lived through plenty of breakups before. Boyfriends came and went.

But Jamie and Caroline? Well, I needed to do whatever it took to win their friendship back. No matter how much they brushed off my apologies, I wouldn't give up until we were all friends again.

I got dressed in jeans and a sweater that was gold—the color of hope—and walked to school, trying to figure out a new approach.

There had to be *something* I could do. Maybe I'd hire a skywriter to scroll an apology over Jamie's house. Maybe I'd have him kidnapped by a deprogrammer who could convince him he still liked me. Maybe he'd need a kidney and I could volunteer to be the donor.

You had to forgive someone if they gave you a kidney, right?

All morning I barely heard what the teachers were saying because my mind was whirling, trying to come up with different strategies. It didn't matter how long it took, I'd keep at Jamie and Caroline until we were friends again. It wasn't like I had anything else to do anyway.

When I got to gym class, Caroline was alone on one of the benches in the locker room, trying to untangle a huge knot in one of her sneaker's shoelaces.

I decided, to hell with it—I was just going to start talking and not stop until she forgave me.

"Okay, you need to listen to me," I said, plopping down on the bench beside her.

She gave a little snort of disgust. "Can you go bother someone else?"

"No. This is ridiculous. You have to know that I would never have intentionally hurt Jamie."

Caroline concentrated harder on her shoelace, yanking on it and inadvertently making the knot tighter.

"You know I'm sorry and wish none of this had happened, right? So can't you just . . . *like* me again?"

From the gym I could hear Ms. Vandermeer blowing her whistle. Caroline gave up on the knot and started shoving her foot into the shoe, still not looking at me.

"Come on, Caro. Stop acting like this, okay?" I pleaded.

"I'm not acting. You completely betrayed Jamie." She stood up, her shoe half on, her foot squashing down the heel. "How are we supposed to trust you now?"

I shook my head, giving up. I turned away from her and was headed out toward the gym when Dana came in.

"Hey, Marit, I heard about what you said to Rick Fielding," she called. "Nice going. About time someone put that jerk in his place."

I smiled at her. "Thanks."

Caroline came up behind me and paused, listening.

"What did she say to Rick?" she asked, sounding more normal than I'd heard her in days.

"She told him off in front of all his friends—and the entire cafeteria," Dana told her. "It was classic."

Caroline looked at me, her expression softening. "You did that?"

I noticed a little twinkle in Dana's eye. "The way I heard it, Rick was making fun of me." She paused. "And Jamie."

"So what did you say?" Caroline asked me.

I shrugged. "I said a lot of things. I think I may have called him an assface."

Caroline stared at me for another second, then pushed past me and went into the gym.

28

I had hoped that maybe I had gotten through to Caroline, but the whole rest of the week she and Jamie were back behind their wall, whispering furiously and ignoring me.

Before I left school on Friday, I stopped in the library. I couldn't face another weekend of bad TV. I searched the shelves until I found a copy of *Lust for Life*, a novel about the life of Vincent van Gogh. If I was going to stay inspired and stop thinking my life was a nightmare, maybe reading this would help me do it.

I took the book home and curled up on my bed to read. It was a little boring at first, but the more I stuck with it, the more I started to like it.

I was halfway through it by the time my eyes started to droop, and I fell asleep with the book open on my pillow.

When I woke up the next morning, I discovered Hilly in my room, trying and failing to be quiet as she rummaged through the cosmetics on the top of my dresser.

"Sorry," she said when she saw me open my eyes. "Do you have any Bioré strips? My skin's so bad I look like a Dalmatian."

I stumbled over to the dresser and found the box for her, then slumped back down on my bed.

"You okay?" Hilly asked, still checking out my makeup selection.

"I guess. I mean, no, I'm not, not at all, but there's nothing that anyone can do about it."

Hilly flopped down on the bed next to me. "Jamie and Caroline still mad at you?"

I nodded. "They hate me, Noah hates me—everybody I *know* hates me. No matter what I do, I keep getting myself in bigger and bigger messes."

"It can't be that bad."

"It is! I'm going to have to finish twelfth grade as a home-school kid, like some backwater militia-style Jesus freak."

Hilly laughed. "You do realize that would send Tom and Elena over the edge. There'd be no one to homeschool you, because our parents would be in straitjackets."

"At least then I could forget about sex and dating and boys altogether."

Hilly nudged her shoulder against mine. "I'm sorry. I was

the one who told you to sleep with Jamie in the first place. This is my fault."

"No, it's not. Really. I did this to myself." I rolled over onto my elbow so I was facing my sister. "I wanted the best of both worlds—sex with someone where it would be safe and easy and romance with a guy who made my knees weak."

"You can still have—"

"The thing is, I don't even care about the sex anymore," I interrupted, collapsing onto my back and staring at the ceiling. "If I never had sex again, it would be fine. I just want my friends back."

Hilly regarded me, her eyebrows raised. "Tell you what," she finally said. "I'm going to go call Thad and cancel our plans tonight, and you and me can have a girl's night in."

"No, don't cancel on him. At least one of us should be in love."

"You sure? 'Cause I'll drop him like a bad habit if you need me to hang out with you."

"I'm okay. But thanks."

"What are big sisters for?" she asked, getting up from the bed and picking up the Bioré box.

"I'm going to miss you when you go away to college in January," I called after her.

She waved a hand dismissively at me as she ambled out of the room. "Are you kidding? Bryn Mawr'll *never* accept me."

I finished the van Gogh book by late afternoon, then

wandered out to the living room. My parents were all dressed up for some function at my mom's hospital, but they exchanged worried looks when they saw me still in my pajamas.

"You guys getting ready to leave?" I asked.

I must have come across a little desperate.

"You know, I never enjoy these shindigs anyway," my dad said. "How about we let your mom go alone, and I'll stay home and keep you company?"

"You don't have to do that. I'm *fine*. I have a whole evening planned. Hilly picked up some DVDs for me, and I'm going to watch movies and make Rice Krispie treats and eat the whole pan."

"I like Rice Krispie treats," Dad said. "And I think it'd be fun to watch movies with you."

"I rented *Dirty Dancing*," I told him, knowing that'd stop him. My parents were even bigger film snobs than Jamie.

Dad hesitated. "Still, if you wanted me to stay . . ."

"And *Dirty Dancing Two: Havana Nights*."

My mom and dad exchanged a look. "Okay, we'll leave our cell phones on," Mom said. "If you need *anything* . . ."

"I won't," I told them. "But thank you."

The box said that Rice Krispie treats need to cool for forty-five minutes before you eat them, but I was picking at them anyway, burning my fingers and blowing on them to get the marshmallow cool enough to eat, when the doorbell rang.

I thought about ignoring it—there was no chance it was for me anyway—but the bell rang again, so I paused the movie and set down the pan of treats. Then I walked over and opened the door.

Jamie was on the other side, a small, cowed smile on his face.

I stared at him for a long minute, uncomfortably reminded of the first time we had sex, when we also started the evening in my doorway, unsure of where exactly we stood.

"Can we talk?" he asked.

"Okay," I answered.

He took a tentative step forward, then stopped just inside the door. "I heard you defended me to Rick Fielding. And I heard you told everyone the truth."

I shrugged. "Rick was saying stuff. It made me mad."

"I can't believe you did that," Jamie said.

I blew out a breath, suddenly so weary it felt like my *bones* were exhausted.

"Why wouldn't I?" I asked him, surprised at how angry I sounded. "No matter how much we were fighting, I never stopped being your friend."

"I know," he said softly. "And I want to be friends again."

I blinked once. Twice.

"You do?" I asked, hardly daring to believe it. "Really?"

Jamie nodded. "But—just friends. Nothing more."

I reached over and touched his hand, curled my fingers around his. "Jamie, I'm sorry I don't like you that way. I wish I could."

He smiled, a little sad. "I'm sorry I do. But I'm trying not to."

He took another step forward, opening his arms and wrapping them around me. The hug was tentative at first but grew stronger, and I felt all the stress and unhappiness of the past few weeks begin to dissolve away.

Caroline appeared in the doorway behind him. She saw us standing there with our arms around each other and rolled her eyes.

"Break it up, people. Because I'm not going down that road again."

Jamie and I laughed and let go of each other. As Caroline walked past me into the house, her eyes met mine, and the apology was exchanged between us plainer than any words could have said.

Jamie finally stepped all the way into the house, far enough for me to close the door behind him.

"Just wanted you to know," he said as I turned to face him, "Noah may be calling you."

My mouth dropped open in shock. "What?"

"I—had a little talk with him. I explained things. I think he understands."

Pop!

My jaw was still hanging open, but I was too stunned to close it.

"You talked to Noah for me," I said, still disbelieving. "But—*why?*"

Jamie shrugged, looking embarrassed. "I want you to be happy. Besides—" he added with a wry grin, "how else am I going to get to see *Kaiidan* on DVD?"

I smiled at him, feeling tears in the corners of my eyes. I hugged him again.

"I really do care about him, Jamie. But are you sure you can, you know, be okay with that?" I asked.

"Maybe not at first." He gave me a small smile. "But I will be."

And I knew I would be too. Because whether Noah and I got back together or not, or had sex or not, it didn't matter. For the first time ever, I felt no pressure.

Jamie followed me into the living room, where Caroline was making short work of the Rice Krispie treats.

She gestured to the TV as she hunted around for the remote control. "So what're we watching?" she asked.

"Uh, *Havana Nights*," I told her.

"Perfect. That cool with you, Jamie?"

Jamie twisted up his face, clearly torn between his loathing of the film and his desire for a happy reunion.

"Um—I have *Amores Perros* in my backpack if anyone would rather—"

247

"No way," Caroline said.

I was about to agree with her, two against one. But then—

"I vote for *Amores perros.*"

They both froze, staring at me in shock.

Jamie was the first to move, raising his hands over his head like a prizefighter.

"Oh my God!" he crowed with delight. "The balance has shifted! The power of right prevails!"

Caroline shook her head. "Nuh-uh. The power of the remote prevails. And I have it!"

Jamie paused a moment, then dove at her, trying desperately to get at the clicker.

I sat back against the couch and grinned.

I felt carbonated, like little bubbles of happiness were fizzing up inside me, pop pop pop!

The last month had been crazy and awful and hard, but maybe, just maybe, I could still end up with everything I wanted—a boyfriend, love, sex. . . .

But the important thing was, I still had my friends.

And really, what more could a girl ask for?

ACKNOWLEDGMENTS

A million thanks to Kristen Pettit, for her genius editing; Eloise Flood and the folks at Razorbill, for taking a chance on this book; Jonathan Pecarsky and Karen Gerwin, for all their hard work; Erika Wallington, Sylvanie Wallington, Herbert A. Jeschke, and Bob Popham, for their love and support; Tim Coleman, Joe Lunievicz, and Mike Malone, for their help with the early drafts; Elizabeth Hulings, Pat Diamond, Bob Bollinger, Stephany Folsom, and Ellen White for their friendship and feedback; and Marit Haahr, for letting me use her name. And extra-special thanks to Karen Black, without whom I'd still be sitting at my kitchen table, stuck on chapter one.

ABOUT THE AUTHOR

Aury Wallington has written for the TV shows *Sex and the City*, *Veronica Mars*, and *Courting Alex*. She lives in Los Angeles with her dog, Tuesday.